"A masterpiece of visionary fiction."

—Barbara Marx Hubbard,

*volution:*

*Potential*

"This gem of a                    nsights
and a profound vis            nann is
sure to stimulate, challenge, and inspire you. Welcome
to a great adventure!"

—Alan Cohen,
author of *A Deep Breath of Life:*
*Daily Inspiration for Heart-Centered Living*

"Illustrates the profound spiritual connections from
the distant past to the present moment . . . electrifying."

—John Davis,
author of *Revelation for Our Time*
*A New Paradigm for the Next Millennium*

"Writing in the narrative tradition of *Ishmael* and *The
Celestine Prophecy*, Hartmann takes us on a lively spiritual
journey to rediscover ancient truths that raise profound
questions about how we live and the moral and intellec-
tual foundations of contemporary Western civilization.
A spiritual primer for those who seek a world that works
for all."

—David C. Korten,
author of *The Post-Corporate World:*
*Life After Capitalism*

# Also by Thom Hartmann

*The Prophet's Way*
*Attention Deficit Disorder: A Different Perception*
*The Last Hours of Ancient Sunlight*
*Focus Your Energy*
*Beyond ADD*
*Best of the DTP Forum*
*Think Fast!*
*Healing ADD*
*ADD Success Stories*

# The Greatest
# Spiritual Secret
# of the Century

# Thom Hartmann

WALSCH
**W**
BOOKS

*an imprint of*
**HAMPTON ROADS**
PUBLISHING COMPANY, INC.

Cover design by Marjoram Productions

For information write:
Hampton Roads Publishing Company, Inc.
1125 Stoney Ridge Road
Charlottesville, VA 22902

Or call: 804-296-2772
FAX: 804-296-5096

e-mail: hrpc@hrpub.com
Web site: http://www.hrpub.com

If you are unable to order this book from your local
bookseller, you may order directly from the publisher.
Quantity discounts for organizations are available.
Call 1-800-766-8009, toll-free.

Library of Congress Catalog Card Number: 99-95403

ISBN 1-57174-166-6

10 9 8 7 6 5 4 3 2

Printed on acid-free paper in Canada

"I only tell my Mysteries to those
who are worthy of my Mysteries."

—Jesus, quoted in the Gospel of Thomas

"Of a truth it is, that your God is
a God of gods, and a Lord of kings,
and a revealer of secrets,
seeing thou couldest reveal this secret."

—Daniel 2:47

# Dedication

*To Stephen & Robin Larsen,*

*awakeners of souls extraordinaire*

# Chapter One

# Fear of Flying

Fired.

Even the word sounded ugly, as if you'd been put in front of a firing squad and shot.

*May as well have been,* Paul Abler thought as he stuffed his hands into the pockets of his black greatcoat and hurried down Madison Avenue. The noises and smells of New York drifted by him as if they didn't exist, he was so absorbed in the memory of ten minutes earlier, in a skyscraper fifty floors above the street, the Managing Editor's corner office of one of the city's daily tabloid newspapers. The office that he'd planned to occupy within five years.

A sharp rectangle of light drew his attention to a storefront window, where he caught a glimpse of himself. At almost six feet tall, he reached the end of the reflection. His dark, almost black hair just touched his

1

collar, with a few rebellious hairs curling over it. His deep brown eyes pierced the glow, adding an intensity that more than a few fellow workers had recently commented on. He was glad he'd decided to walk a couple of miles each day. It gave him a firmness that felt natural, rather than the bulging muscles that some of his co-workers had worked so hard at producing in all the so-called "right" places.

Although the phrase used was "laid off," Paul—in the interests of journalistic integrity and knowing what it meant for his career—preferred to use and think of it as what it was: fired.

Paul had stood opposite the massive, paper-strewn desk of Mack Kessler, managing editor of *The New York Daily Tribune.* Another desk, perpendicular to the first, held the computers that linked the M.E. into the newspaper's intranet. Mack liked to pretend he lived in the days when newspapers were about news and editors smoked cigars and snarled a lot. In fact, he was a tall, Yale-educated, 36-year-old yuppie who wore two-hundred-dollar ties, surfed the 'net, and worked out three days a week at The Reebok Sports Club, where the membership cost more than Paul's last car.

Still, Mack was older than Paul's 29 years. Paul had finished his M.A. in journalism five years earlier, spent a year in the "intern" slave-labor camps, a year as an editorial assistant, two years ago got a job as a *real* reporter for a *real* local daily newspaper in upstate New York, and eleven months ago landed this position in the Big Apple at the *Tribune.* Finally, a reporter for a New York City newspaper. Maybe in another few years–if he could break some really big stories–he could even get a job with the *Times.* He'd planned a great future in journalism, and he'd kept on track.

Until now.

So there stood Mack, who loved to give speeches about how important investigative journalism is to a free society, telling Paul that he's been laid off, along with fourteen other employees.

"This is really because I offended an advertiser," Paul had said.

"No, Paul," Mack had said, back in his office after the brief meeting in the conference room where Paul and the other fourteen people had been summoned. Paul was the only reporter in the bunch; the rest were all support staff or in administration. "This is because the owners of the newspaper think we can operate more efficiently with a leaner staff."

"More profitably, you mean."

"I'm sure the stockholders would applaud that, as would the American public. This is not a scandal, Paul. Layoffs happen every day of the week, all across the world."

"But we both know there are other reporters here

who are not as competent as I am," Paul said. "I was picked because of the London story."

"Actually," Mack said, his fingers nervously tapping the top of his desk as if he was planning to bolt from the room at any moment, "I think it's because some of the others here think you're too hungry. The London story was just a symptom. You're driven, Paul. Success at any cost, win that Pulitzer next week. I think you've scared the wits out of some of the people above me. You've also made enemies of your fellow reporters. They think you're a rogue, a cowboy."

Paul leaned forward and, his voice fluid with acid, said, "You're saying I'm canned because I'm *too good*?"

"Too driven, Paul. You work fifteen hours a day, seven days a week. You pour everything you have into your work, and there's nothing left over for you or anybody else. Speaking as a friend, I don't think it's healthy."

Paul shook his head, knowing Mack was no friend and never would be. "Too good. I work too hard, and that scares the ones who just want to get by." *Like Mack,* Paul thought. *He knows I'd have his job in a year or two if I played it right.*

"Of course, I'd deny it," Mack said, "but everybody knows anyway. Layoffs are opportunities for people to settle political scores and consolidate their empires. You frightened my boss, the way you charged into that London story without even consulting anybody." His tone softened. "I'm just sorry you weren't here long enough to earn a severance package. But I guess it's better for the company this way. We'll pay you through the end of the week, although you have to clean out your desk and leave now."

"This isn't right," Paul had said, but he knew as he said it that Mack wasn't interested—the transnational corporation that owned the *Tribune* wasn't interested—in the story he'd uncovered about a London company that was bribing New York politicians to get tax breaks and government business. A London company with a division that advertised heavily in the New York newspapers. And, he'd discovered, the *Tribune* wouldn't defend him for the furor he'd stirred up just *investigating* the yet-unpublished story. If anything, Mack had pointed out, it reflected poorly on the paper; newspapers don't take on the corporate big guys if they want to survive in the business. They haven't in at least two decades. Reporters shouldn't poke into corners without the lawyers and corporate owners first telling them it's safe territory. And they should never upstage their own editors.

Mack reached over to the bowl full of different-colored Bic lighters that sat on his desk. He smoked, and was constantly losing lighters, so he kept a good supply. He picked up a red one and tossed it to Paul by way of ending the conversation. "Here, kid. Set the world on fire. And turn in your ID to Cynthia at the front desk on the way out."

And so Paul Abler, unemployed and alone, marched through the cold February streets of Manhattan, the wind whipping dust and auto exhaust through his thick brown hair. The sky was a low, gray boil of clouds, threatening snow as the temperature hovered one or two degrees below the freezing point.

*I've got about two weeks to find something,* Paul thought, glancing down at the overcoat that had set him back eighteen hundred dollars at Saks Fifth Avenue.

When he got the job with the *Tribune,* he'd immediately gone out and spent almost four thousand dollars on clothes. He soon discovered that the jeans and white shirt he was currently wearing were all he needed, but still, he'd told himself, he needed to be ready to be well dressed. And, truth be told, he had used the two suits he bought to good advantage when he'd been investigating the London company's shady dealings. The clothes got him taken seriously by secretaries and underlings, and even convinced one guy he "might" be a senior assistant to one of New York's senators.

But they cost a fortune, relatively, and he'd gone a month late on his rent to pay for them, and that added to the cost of lunches and taxis. Before he knew it he'd pushed his credit cards to the point where he couldn't get any more cash advances on them, and was now two months behind on his rent. The pay-now-or-we'll-evict-you notice had been stuck under his door three days ago.

Fired, broke, and in debt. A week, maybe two, to come up with his back rent, or he'd be on the streets. And no job reference; who in journalism would hire somebody fired by the *Tribune*? If he couldn't make it in a mid-level tabloid, his chances with the *Times* or *The Washington Post* were shot. His professors had lied to him; they hadn't worked in the business for years; most probably had never left the comfortable world of Academe. A reporter's first commitment isn't to the truth, or to his readers, or to the public good; it's to the corporations who pay the bills. Unless there's a war—which is profitable to the defense contractors, which include the owners of some of the nation's largest news outlets—a reporter no longer has any chance to break a really big story because so much is now off-limits. Why hadn't they just told him that when he was a freshman, so he could get out and go into something where people were honest about climbing and making money, like a stock brokerage? Instead, he'd bought the myth of Woodward and Bernstein, the lie that said if you work hard and tell the truth, damn the consequences, no matter how it shakes up the world, you'll come out rich and famous in the end.

The liars.

He saw a pay phone just before the next corner and stopped at it, dropped in the right change, and dialed

Susan's direct number at work. They'd been dating on a pretty regular basis for about eight months, and in the past few months Paul had slept over at her apartment, or her at his, most weekends. He took that as a good sign that she was serious about the relationship, although she disliked discussing—or "overanalyzing," as she called it—their future.

"Susan Gordon," she answered, in that business-like tone that told the caller he'd reached an advertising copywriter at one of the largest advertising agencies in the world. Big-shot-by-association was what Paul had called it once, offending Susan to the point where he'd had to spend two days apologizing. She finally forgave him when he sent flowers to her office.

"Hi, Susan," Paul said. "How's your day?"

"It sucks, like usual," she said in a tired voice. "Sometimes I think everybody in the cosmetics industry is insane. They all have delusions of grandeur."

"The perfume campaign giving you fits?"

"You wouldn't believe," she said. "I hear traffic. Are you calling from the street?"

"Yeah," Paul said. "I'm on Madison, just north of forty-fourth. I had a bit of a falling-out with Mack."

"A falling out?" There was a subtle but unmistakable shift in her tone, an implied disapproval.

"He said I was working too hard and had made some enemies. He tried to say it was just a corporate downsize, then said it was because of that London story. I think what it's really about, though, is that he thinks I was after his job. If I could have gotten that story into print, I would have been the hottest reporter in New York in the past two years."

"And?" She drew it out.

"And so I kept working on it, on my own time, and he fired me."

"You're kidding."

"Well, I suppose I could say that I was laid off, but the truth is they fired me. I don't suppose it makes much difference."

"It makes all the difference in the world, Paul," she said, her voice soft as if she were talking to a child.

"I'll find something else," he said.

"Is this going to be the pattern of your life?" she said. "Holding a job for a year and then getting canned?"

"No, really, this was a serious issue. No editor should be willing to compromise . . ."

"Paul, this is the real world!" Her voice was thick and low. "It's *business*. It's all about compromise. Work your butt off if you want, climb as high as you can, I know how important that is to you. But don't embarrass the wrong people."

"No, it's about journalism, not business. It's an entirely different thing."

"What, you think newspapers are in the truth business?

Is that how they stay in business? Paul, I think your ambition has blinded you to the fact that it's the advertisers who are paying your salary. You're in such a hurry to make it to the top that you're losing perspective. These aren't the old days. The corporations have taken over."

An ambulance with its siren on snaked its way up Madison Avenue, and he put his hand over his left ear so he could hear the phone. "I think I was just working too hard, doing too much. I was a threat to the other reporters, even to Mack, because I was showing them up as lazy . . ."

"Paul!" Her voice rose over the sound of the siren, and Paul felt his heart sink. "Listen to you!" she shouted. "Maybe they want to have a life, but you're willing to throw everything over the edge just to be the next Bob Woodward."

"Maybe I can get a job with one of the news magazines . . ."

"And maybe they'll have no interest whatsoever in hiring somebody who doesn't understand the realities of teamwork and cooperation in the twenty-first century corporate world. You know what they call workaholics in the business world?"

"Powerful and wealthy is what I'd call them . . ." He felt like he was talking to a stranger, the change in her tone had been so rapid.

"*Alone*, that's what," she said, her tone cutting. She took a deep and loud breath. "Paul, you don't have to end up all alone at the top. You're incredibly talented. But you've got to slow down and learn to play on a team."

"But a team doesn't win a Pulitzer, a reporter does . . ."

The ambulance faded into the distance, and her voice was again clear and crisp through the cold black plastic he held to his ear. "I know." Her tone softened. "And I understand how important that is to you."

"Would you like to get together tonight?"

There was a pause, and he could hear her breathe. Then she said, "I have a pile of work I have to take home tonight, Paul. I'm sorry."

"Tomorrow?"

"Tomorrow is Friday, and I have a date with a girl-friend to see a show that's playing off-Broadway. Her sister is in it."

"This weekend?"

"It's really not gonna be a good weekend for me," she said.

"I understand," he said, his vision blurring in the cold wind on his face. "I'll call you next week."

"You do that," she said. "And have a great weekend." Her voice had a forced perkiness to it.

The line clicked; his coins dropped into the bowels of the phone, and a dial tone filled his ear. Paul looked at the receiver as if seeing it for the first time, his stomach feeling like he'd been punched, and slowly hung up the phone. "Good bye to you, too," he said softly, as the receiver fell into the cradle.

He turned and stepped back into the flow of people on the busy afternoon street. *She was only a friend,* he said over and over in his mind. And then, *It was just a casual relationship, even though I'd hoped for more. She couldn't have helped my career, and wasn't really interested in my future. She has her own career to worry about.*

A block down, along Madison Avenue between 43rd and 42nd streets, he started to walk by a large bear of a man with neatly-cut black hair and a thick black beard, wearing a red-and-black plaid winter hunting coat and green army pants stuffed into tall black boots. The man stepped in front of him and abruptly established eye contact. Instinctively, Paul started to look away—eye contact in Manhattan can be dangerous, a lesson he'd learned well in his three years living there—but the man grabbed his right arm at the bicep and said in a loud voice, "Are you going to heaven, brother?"

"What?" Paul said, compounding his eye-contact mistake by violating Manhattan's unspoken, never-respond-to-them rule. He immediately realized his mistake and tried to pull his arm from the man's grip.

But the man held him tightly, the bond forged by Paul's response, and said, "I mean are you saved?

Have you accepted Jesus Christ as your personal Lord and Savior?"

Paul felt a return flush of the resentment and bellicosity he'd experienced just ten minutes earlier in Mack's office. Who the hell did Mack think he was, telling Paul that a reporter shouldn't report the news if it made a big company uncomfortable? And who the hell did this guy think he was asking if Paul was "saved"?

"Is that what I have to do to get into heaven?" Paul said to the guy, his voice trembling with outrage, as if the man were a stand-in for the hypocritical Mack who'd just shattered his life.

"Accept, believe, be forgiven, and repent!" the man proclaimed, raising the index finger of his free right hand in the air. "And you'll spend eternity in heaven!"

"Lemme get this straight," Paul said. "If I do these things, then I go to heaven when I die?"

"Right! An eternal paradise!"

"And you're going to be there, too?"

"Of course!" the man roared.

Paul laughed, what he knew was a sarcastic and cutting laugh, and said: "If that's where you're going, then I think I'd rather be somewhere else."

He pulled away from the shocked man's grip and continued his walk down Madison Avenue.

"You'll burn in hell forever!" the man shouted at his back. "You're running scared and you better be scared, because you're gonna die in sin and burn in hell! The God of Abraham, Isaac, and Jacob will get you, because he's wrathful and jealous! That's right—run away. You can run, but you can't hide!" The man's voice, his rant, faded into the sounds of traffic as Paul kept walking briskly down Madison, along with the sea of other people all pretending to be totally oblivious to the man shouting threats behind them.

But as he walked, Paul remembered his teenage years, the time he'd gone to Billy Graham's sermon at Shea Stadium and walked down front for the altar call, and the church he briefly attended after that, where the pastor's favorite theme was original sin and damnation. He eventually stopped attending the church, to a gnawing feeling of guilt.

*What does it all mean?* he wondered as he walked. *Was everybody born evil and hated by God because of a mistake some now-dead woman made thousands of years ago? Was it possible? Would any father, even a Heavenly Father, torture and murder his own son to save the people he created from his own wrath? Could it really be that this was the purpose of life, to escape the wrath of the one who created us? Or is there something deeper, something more comprehensible, something more compassionate, perhaps even right there in the Bible?*

"I'd give anything to know the answer to that one," Paul said from his heart, half aloud, a little corner of his mind also thinking that it would be a reporter's ultimate story. He caught himself, wondering if any of the people around had heard him talking to himself. He looked around cautiously as he stopped with the flow of people for the red light at 41$^{st}$ Street, but nobody seemed to have noticed his lapse. Or, if they had, they were obeying Rule One of life in New York: avoid eye contact.

As he was scanning the crowd, he glanced across the street and froze in shock. For a terrible moment, he watched in horror as a little girl, perhaps five years old, broke the grip of her mother's hand on the other side of the street and dashed into the crosswalk. A delivery truck roared down the street, intending to run through his green light full-bore.

The girl's mother screamed, people gasped, and Paul awoke from his trance. *She'll die if I don't do something,* he knew. Nobody was moving: the scene was eerily in slow motion. Looking at the child again, he swallowed and surged into the intersection.

Three steps out, the voice in his head was now shouting, *you're gonna die,* but he didn't stop. Just five more steps and he could shove the little girl—now frozen in horror staring at the truck, whose brakes were screeching—hard enough to knock her out of the way. One step, then another, lunging forward, his hands stretched out in front of him, his mind racing as he calculated the odds that he could get there fast enough and shove the girl hard enough to knock her out of the way. If he succeeded, he would then, himself, be in front of the truck that he knew would take his life. But even if he wanted to turn back, he'd already gone too fast and too far.

And then he was flying.

*Somebody must have pushed me really hard*, he thought, as his motion through the air blurred. It almost felt as if strong arms had lifted him up under his chest and the tops of his legs, as if somebody were holding him the way he'd held kids in the summer camp pool where he'd taught swimming. And then he was rushing forward, his own hands outstretched like Superman, his feet no longer on the ground from the force of the shove. He grabbed the little girl and sailed with her on past the truck, feeling its bumper nick the heel of his right shoe.

The momentum was gone, and he fell to the ground in a pile, his cheek and fingers skinned, as the screaming little girl landed on her feet and ran into her mother's arms.

"That was one hell of a save!" a fiftyish man in a tan trench coat said, his voice filled with wonder, as he helped Paul to his feet. "Just like Mel Gibson, something in the movies!"

Paul looked down at his scraped-up right hand and brushed the dirt from it, then shook out his coat. "Did you see who shoved me?" he said, catching his breath.

Several people had stepped back from him, not willing or interested enough to get involved. The woman with her little girl, now sobbing softly, ran up to Paul and squeezed his arm, a thankful gesture, and said, "Thank you for saving my daughter's life. You're a good man."

"You're welcome," Paul said. "But I think I had some help. Did you see who pushed me?"

She shook her head. "All I could do was stare at my daughter and scream. You took such a chance for her."

"I'm glad I could help," Paul said.

She pecked his cheek with a kiss and, embarrassed, turned and walked away with her daughter in tow.

The light changed, the crowd flowed away like a river. The man in the tan coat, his hair combed up and over his baldness, shook his head and said, "That was one hell of a jump you made, to fly like that. You a professional athlete?"

"I didn't jump," Paul said. "Somebody shoved me."

The man shrugged and walked off, leaving Paul shivering in the cold wind.

## Chapter Two

# Ready for the Rains?

Paul Abler's apartment was on the twenty-first (and top) floor of a brick apartment building near Madison Square Garden, in that part of Manhattan known as Chelsea. It was a co-op built by the Garment Worker's Union in the late 1950s.

Paul took his time, walking the mile-and-a-quarter from where he'd saved the child to his apartment, stopping along the way to buy a slice of pizza, browsing store windows. He alternated between feelings of despair at his financial, relationship, and employment situation, and attempts to convince himself that he now had a new lifetime of opportunities ahead of him in all three areas. Part of him knew it was happy-talk, but another part also knew there was a grain of truth to it. Maybe there was something out there waiting for him that was better than working as a drone in a multinational's make-believe world of what they cynically called "news." Maybe there was a woman out there who'd be more loving and less judgmental than Susan. Maybe life could get better now, and would.

He used his key to open the building's front door, walked into the lobby, and nodded at Billy, the retired cop the building hired as a combination security and maintenance man. Billy glanced at Paul's scraped face and hand, and turned his gray eyes to look out the window onto Eighth Avenue. New Yorkers learn not to ask questions.

During his walk home, a plan had formed in Paul's mind. A short-term plan, granted, but at least it may stave off the eviction notice and keep his credit cards from being cancelled. With that plan in mind, he'd purposely taken his time getting home to arrive just after five.

In the apartment next to Paul's, which shared a partitioned balcony with his apartment looking up Eighth Avenue, lived Rich Whitehead, lawyer extraordinaire. Rich shared Paul's desire to make it big in the Big Apple, but was hindered by an overabundance of what Paul thought of as lust. Rich, of course, called it his love life, or conquest, or, in his more exuberant (and vodka-soaked) moments, "My contribution to making the world a better and more loving place!"

What it all meant was that Rich had gone to Columbia

University's law school specifically and only to be able to join one of New York's largest corporate law firms to get enough money and recognition that there would be an unending stream of women clamoring for his attention. He had the very explicit goal of working his way up the firm's ladder to the point where his income would exceed a million dollars a year, which would support a Hugh Hefner lifestyle. A partnership in the firm would be nice, too, of course, but Rich understood that that was at least twenty years into the future. But doing M & A work—corporate mergers and acquisitions—was incredibly profitable for the attorneys involved, particularly when you could find and publicize dirt on the company to be taken over, thus driving its price through the floor. And sometimes the acquiring companies would even offer the lawyers working on their cases ground-floor opportunities. The success stories Rich told—usually when his mistress-of-the-week was in hearing range—were extraordinary, although Rich was still in the building, so his income clearly hadn't yet hit his goals.

In his five years with the firm, Rich's power had grown to the point where he currently presided over an empire of two junior lawyers, a paralegal, a clerk, and two secretaries. He passed out thousands of dollars a week in paychecks, and had told Paul many times that he was on the cusp of making Big Money himself.

Maybe, Paul thought, Rich could use a good writer. It could tide him over while he sent out résumés to newspapers around the country and hit *Time* and *Newsweek.*

Paul walked to the elevator, took it up to the twenty-first floor, and knocked on the door next to his own. A moment later the peephole flickered, then Paul heard the sound of the three locks being undone and the door pulled open to reveal Rich, standing in a dark-blue terrycloth bathrobe and holding a glass with ice cubes and a clear liquid. He stood a half-foot taller than Paul at about six foot six, with a large barrel-shaped middle. He wore gold wire-rimmed glasses and his pale blue eyes were exaggerated in the thick lenses. Rich's hair was short and corporate, but still an unruly mass of light brown waves.

"Hi, Paul," Rich said, a touch of reserve in his voice that Paul took to imply he'd interrupted something. "What's up?" He glanced at the abraded side of Paul's face and added, "What happened to you?"

"Oh, nothing," said Paul. "I fell on the street, up on Madison. Pushed some kid out of the way of a truck."

"Playing the hero?" Rich smiled. "Maybe we should sue the trucker."

Paul smiled and shrugged. "It was really no big deal. Got a minute? This won't take long."

Rich stepped back and waved into the room. "Come right in."

Paul walked into Rich's living room, which was decorated in black leather, glass, and chrome. It smelled of pot and shampoo and leather. Signed Dali prints adorned the walls, and the carpet was a startling pure eggshell white. A big-screen TV dominated the far corner, near the window out over the balcony, and in a chair next to it sat a stunning blonde woman, wearing only a silk bathrobe with a dragon embroidered down one side. Her hair was damp, and she looked like she was in her very early twenties. She looked Paul up and down quickly, and turned on a professional smile, all teeth and eyes, and said, "Hi!"

Flustered, Paul said, "Hi," and turned to Rich. "I didn't realize you had company . . ."

"No problem," Rich interrupted. "Paul, this is Cheryl. Cheryl, Paul. Paul is my next-door neighbor, a hot-shot reporter for the *Tribune*." He turned to Paul and said, "Cheryl is a model and student at FIT." FIT, Paul knew, was the Fashion Institute of Technology, just down the block at 27th Street between Seventh and Eighth Avenues, and a magnet that drew beautiful women from all over the world . . . a fact not lost on Rich when he was deciding where in Manhattan to live. Plus, the neighborhood was experiencing a bit of a renaissance, with lots of trendy restaurants, bars, clubs, and shops opening. Great places to meet the women from FIT.

Rich sat down in a chair next to Cheryl, and gestured Paul to the black leather couch that faced the window. "Would you like a drink?"

"I think I'll pass," Paul said. "I don't want to interrupt you two . . ."

"We just took a shower," Rich said with a wink. "I've got to head back to the office in a few hours, so we're going to dinner at Krour Thai after this drink." Defining the parameters of the time available to Paul, which was to say very little.

"Well," Paul said, "I left the *Tribune* today."

"Hey!" Rich said, standing up and saluting with his glass. "Congratulations!" He took a sip, while Cheryl watched with a Siamese-cat expression on her face. Paul often wondered who was the user and who was the used; the women Rich picked up often seemed far more intelligent—or at least far wiser—than Rich himself.

"Yeah, well, it wasn't something I'd probably have chosen. We had a disagreement about the meaning of the phrase 'work ethic.'"

Rich raised his right eyebrow. "They thought seventy hours a week was too little?"

"They thought it was too much. I was making people nervous."

"Ah, so. Same in the law. Build your alliances first, line up your allies. Establish your empire. Then you go for the jugular." Rich sat back down, nodding his head like a wise old man who'd seen it all. "So now you've learned a good lesson and you're free for a new beginning."

"I guess so. Somewhere out there is a newspaper who's not afraid to hire a *real* investigative reporter. In the meantime, though, I'm a little tight, cash-wise. So I was wondering if you knew of any opportunities at your firm for part-time work. I'm a pretty competent wordsmith."

Rich glanced at Cheryl, who smiled back at him, then took a long, slow sip of his drink. "You know, the Russians make the best vodka in the world," he said. "And the worst. The secret, of course, is knowing which is which."

Paul nodded, having heard many times Rich's story of when the firm sent him to Moscow and he learned All About Vodka And Russian Women.

"Anyhow," Rich continued, "I don't know. I'll ask around. Sometimes we hire temps or freelancers, although usually they're paralegals or lawyers who just work on the side, if you know what I mean."

"I figured . . ."

"But I'll check it out!" Rich said with a decisive tone, standing again. "I'll certainly check it out and get back with you."

Paul caught the cue and stood up, allowing himself to be guided to the door with Rich's arm reaching over his shoulder, murmuring reassurances until Paul was back in the hallway and the door was closed.

Paul turned and walked to his own apartment's door, used one key on the dead-bolt lock, the other on the doorknob lock, pushed the door open and walked in.

As familiar as the apartment was to him, Paul still noted the contrast between his place and Rich's. His was considerably less elegant, with simple light brown carpet, two tan fabric sofas—one long and the other short—an easy chair, and a ten-year-old faux teak wall unit that held his TV, stereo, and books. He walked through the living room to the kitchen, poured himself a glass of white wine from the refrigerator, and went back to the living room, noticing that he was limping slightly. His muscles ached. As he reached for the TV remote control to check the day's news, he heard a knock at the door, a rapid and forceful rap-rap-rap. He stopped in mid-reach and carried his wine-glass to the door. Pulling aside the cover to the peephole, he saw an old man in a brown tweed jacket. The fellow looked to be in his seventies, with trim white hair and beard, his jacket middle-buttoned formally over his tie, holding a clipboard. He was smiling broadly.

Paul opened the door. "Yes?"

"Hello, young man," the gentleman said. "You're Paul Abler, and I have a few questions for you, if you don't mind. I'm doing a survey." There was a faint accent to his English, a guttural quality shared by Middle-Easterners and Slavic people.

"I've had a really miserable day," Paul said, thinking the man must have gotten his name off the mailbox downstairs, probably had followed somebody into the building to get past the front-door lock. "Maybe another time."

"I hate to press, but if you answer these questions, there's a real premium at the end of this. Believe me, this is not a gift you want to say 'no' to. Much larger than anything you can imagine." Paul saw the man's eyes glance over his scratched face, the dirt and tear on the collar of his white shirt, and a small smile—perhaps a smile of sympathy—came to the man's face. "You look like you could use a gift."

"I'm fine . . ." Paul began, recognizing the old door-to-door ploy and preparing to close the door on the man. But the man's smile reminded him of the summer he'd spent during his first year of college selling magazines door to door, paid on commission, and all the doors that were slammed in his face. How he kept trying to smile at all the fearful or angry or apathetic people who wouldn't even listen to how he could get them their first year's subscription for free if they'd just sign up for two years. And they almost never smiled back. It was a miserable job, and when the end of the summer came he was relieved to get back to college. It was his first solid realization of how cold and uncaring people could behave toward strangers. He felt the door-knob, cool in his hand, and pulled it further open, thinking, *I was fired today; the last thing I should be doing is making somebody else's job harder.* "What the heck," he said. "Come on in."

The man followed Paul into the living room, closing the door behind him, and walked to the short sofa under the window that looked up Eighth Avenue. "May I sit down for a moment?" he said.

"Sure," Paul said, sitting on the longer couch, diagonal to the man. The pizza had upset his stomach, and he was thinking of taking a couple of aspirin and letting himself turn into a TV zombie with the remote control in one hand and the glass of wine in the other. It was a rare indulgence, but sounded appealing; as soon as the salesman left. He added, "But let's try to get this over with quickly, ok?"

"Of course," the man said, with a glance to his clipboard. "The first question is, 'Do you believe in God?'"

Paul remembered the evangelist on the street earlier and felt a flush of anger. "Are you from some church or cult?"

"Oh, heavens no," the man said, his brown eyes twinkling, smile lines showing around them. "This is for the Wisdom School."

The smile disarmed Paul. "What's that?"

The man got a momentary faraway look in his eyes, then looked back at Paul. "Every hundred years or so, when the secret seems the most lost, some people will step forward and share it again with the world. That's our work."

"Sounds like a cult to me," Paul said.

The man shrugged. "I'm not here to recruit you. You asked for this."

"That's a joke."

"No," the man said. "It's serious. You asked right after you so deftly handled that evangelist on the street this morning."

Paul thought back and felt a moment of disorientation as he remembered his half-whispered comment that he wished he knew the answers to the spiritual questions that had haunted him since childhood. He looked at the man and heard his own voice drop as he said, "You were standing beside me on the street?"

"After a fashion," the man said, smiling. His smile seemed so heartfelt and genuine, like Paul, when he was a child, had imagined Santa Claus would look.

"I don't get it," Paul said. "This is too weird, and I'm thinking that no matter how hard door-to-door selling is, I shouldn't have let you in. You followed me here."

"Well, yes, after I gave you a little bit of help."

"Help?"

"Saving that little girl." The man's face turned serious. "That was a noble decision, Paul, but I could see that you weren't going to make it. And I saw that you were willing to give up your life to try. That's what I saw, and I couldn't let that happen. So I decided to carry you across."

Paul took a quick sip of his wine, and the memory of the experience in the intersection washed back over him. "You're the one who shoved me?"

"No," the man said, shaking his head. "I didn't shove you."

"Then how did you help?"

"I picked you up and carried you."

"You what?"

"You felt my arms under your chest and legs, didn't you?"

Paul paused, feeling out of breath, remembering the sensation of the strong arms holding him up and propelling him through the intersection. "But I didn't see anything."

Suddenly the couch was empty, and Paul gasped. There was a small depression in the cushion where the man had been sitting. "Nor do you see anything now," the man's voice came from the air.

Paul looked at the empty sofa and considered the frightening possibility that working too hard, sleeping too little, and being fired had finally pushed him over the edge into total insanity. *This must be what it's like*, he thought. *First you hallucinate, just like those people who have voices in their heads. Then you do awful things because the voices tell you that you must . . .*

"You're not imagining this," the man said as he slowly reappeared. Now he had shoulder-length graying hair and a much fuller beard, and was dressed in a white toga or tunic, his legs bare, his feet in worn leather sandals. "It's very real. You saved that little girl's life, and I saved yours."

Paul downed half the glass of wine in a good-sized gulp and felt it first cool, then warm his stomach. He blinked hard, half expecting his hallucination to be gone, but the man was still there. He looked at the man's face, which was now sun-darkened and lined with age-wrinkles. His eyes were a dark brown, almost black, and his arms and legs had the ropy, muscular quality of a person who has performed decades of hard physical work.

"Who *are* you?" Paul said.

The man nodded. "An important question," he said. "At least in your time and place." His voice was soft and reassuring, deep and rumbling as if it came from an antediluvian cistern. "But first, confirm for me that you felt me carry you through that intersection. That you know this is the truth, what I am saying."

Paul looked at his glass, lifted it to his lips, and took another large swallow. Turbulence churned his stomach, and the abrasions on his face and hand ached. He could hear the faint sound of traffic outside, a click and whir as the refrigerator in the kitchen cycled on, the creak of heated water expanding the radiator behind the man's sofa. Through the wall, he could faintly hear the thumping bass of Rich's stereo. "Yes," Paul said, remembering flying through the air across the street. "Perhaps I felt something. It was you?"

"Yes. You may call me Noah."

Paul lifted his eyebrows and said, "Like the ark?"

"The very same."

"How'd you know my name? How did you pick me up this afternoon without my seeing you? Who *are* you?"

Noah stretched his arms out and put large, gnarled hands on either side of the back of the sofa. "I'm the first of your teachers. You have been accepted into the Wisdom School."

"What is that?"

Noah ran his fingers through the hair over his ears. "The oldest Wisdom Schools go back into antiquity. They're grounded in the priestly and shamanic mentorships that exist even to this day among the world's Older Cultures. When the earliest dominators, or kings, built the city/states, the Wisdom Schools came into being as a way of preserving the Older Culture wisdom against the onslaught of the modern, or Younger

Culture. The tradition has survived in many ways. Early Christianity was a Wisdom School before one faction of it was taken over and promoted to primacy by the Roman Empire. When it became the official state religion, the Secret had to be buried, layered over with confusion. People were told that it wasn't really what Jesus said, or what the Jewish prophets before him said, that the Secret was really just some nice words."

"What does the Wisdom School teach?"

"You know how Saint Francis and Saint John of the Cross and Martin Buber and Meister Eckhard and Rumi were all scorned by the mainstream church people of their times? They were called heretics and worse?"

"I remember something like that in college. Studying the history of the world's religions."

"They were all mystics, as were the founders of all the world's great religions," Noah said. "They understood the mysteries, and each one *lived* the Secret. Some mystics gain recognition in their time, others not until years after their deaths, and most are forever anonymous. But all walked through their time on Earth with an incredible power and knowledge and insight, which, to the average person, seems almost incomprehensible. This knowledge is now offered to you. I am here to begin your training."

"Are you some kind of preacher?"

Noah shook his head. "Different people and different

cultures have different names for what and who I am. The original people of North America called us shape-shifters. The ancient Greeks and Romans called us gods and goddesses, many of the Semitic tribes called us prophets, and modern Europeans and Americans call us ghosts, spirits, or angels. But you can call me 'friend.'"

Paul's breath caught in his throat, as he remembered the feeling of the arms under him, then the sight of the bearded man vanishing and reappearing on the sofa. "You're an angel . . ."

Noah interrupted him with a laugh. "I prefer ghost. It better captures, at least in English, my nature. 'Angel' implies that I'm associated with some particular religion or belief system. Ghost is more generic: every culture in the world knows about ghosts."

"You're the ghost of Noah? Like in the ark?"

Noah shrugged. "I'm most comfortable with this body, this name. I first used it during the time of the end of the last ice age, when the oceans rose and many of my people drowned. My story was told over and over again, and eventually that brought me back into this world."

Paul jumped up from the sofa and took another swallow of his wine. "This is too weird," he said. "I've never believed in all this supernatural stuff. I think the stress I've been under has popped my mind."

Noah vanished again. Paul spun around, but the room was empty and this time there wasn't even the slight depression on the brown faux-velvet fabric of the sofa. "What . . ."

"It's real, Paul; I'm still here," Noah's voice came, and he appeared in a blink by the door into the kitchen. "Of course I could just as easily be in Hong Kong. Even right now as I'm here."

"That's impossible."

"But you went to Sunday school."

"Yeah, but . . ."

"Did you think it possible that Jesus was speaking the truth when He said, 'These things I have done, you shall do also, and even greater things than these'? In both the Old and New Testament are stories of people doing what I do. And in the Upanishads and the Vedas and the Koran, and in the oral history of every people in the world, in all of human history. Do you think that is an accident or mistake?"

"But you're a ghost or an angel or whatever . . ."

"That's beside the point. We'll talk about that later. I learned the Secret and once saved the world–my world–and now it's your opportunity."

Paul sat back down on the sofa with a thud and rubbed the left side of his face that wasn't scratched up. "Me?" he said. His voice sounded faint and unreal in his own head. "You've gotta be kidding."

"No, I'm serious. You're enrolled in the Wisdom School. You've been enrolled, in fact, since before your birth. It's why you chose this life, this body, this time. It all led to this. And then you called out today, so now I'm here and this is your big opportunity."

"But I'm just a reporter. I snoop out stories and break the news. I'd hardly say that qualifies me to save the world."

"Each person has the potential. I'm here to tell you, to show you, yours. Surely you've had that intuition all your life that your destiny is a great and important one?"

Paul paused, then said, "Yes, but I also dismissed that as an ego trip. I wanted to win the Pulitzer prize."

"It's what drew you into journalism, what draws so many other people into their lines of work. Even an office worker, a construction worker, can save the world, one person at a time. Every person can. And you chose before you were born to do this work in a very large way."

"I chose my destiny?"

"Many people do. And your destiny is to live and share the message that will save the world."

"How?"

"First, you must learn the Greatest Spiritual Secret of the Century. Then you use the skills you've been refining all your life to tell the world, and then things will change. Think of it as the biggest scoop of your life."

"The Greatest Spiritual Secret of the Century?" Paul could hear his own voice rising. The wine was calming him, but he also knew he needed a clear head for whatever was going on, whether it was all a hallucination or was true. He put the glass on the coffee table in front of the couch. "You mean like in a hundred years, the greatest secret?"

Noah walked over to the couch and sat back down. "Actually, you could say it's the greatest secret of all time. And, it's so much *not* a secret that it's astounding. Any shaman in the world will tell you, every prophet has said it, Jesus told people about it. It's being shouted at your world every day by the few tribes remaining in the rain forests and jungles and plains, as your culture destroys their homes and your oxygen supply. Six and seven thousand years ago, the founders of Hinduism were writing about it. Five and then four thousand years ago the Hebrew prophets told it, and then Buddha almost three thousand years ago, and Jesus two thousand years ago, and Mohammed in the past thousand years, and now you have the opportunity to learn it. All over again. Every few centuries it visits us again, the same message but often cloaked in different-seeming words or metaphors. But, oddly, most people can't imagine it could be possible, or don't hear it, or the institutions that have taken over the organized religions bury it in so many layers of nonsense that it seems lost."

It reminded Paul of the discussions he'd had with his friend, Thomas, in college. What is the meaning of life?

What is the difference between spirituality and religion? What is faith? Who made the world, and why, and how? And why are we here? Somehow those questions had all been lost in his drive to become a star reporter.

"So," Paul said, using his reporter's tone, "What is this Greatest Spiritual Secret of the Century?"

Noah smiled. "If I simply told it to you in one sentence—which I could do, because it's only four words long—you wouldn't understand, just as virtually your entire culture, the entire world, does not understand. So I am the first of three Wisdom School teachers who have been sent to give you what you must first know, so you can ultimately understand the true meaning of the Secret and become a Wisdom School teacher, yourself." He paused for a moment, then said, "I will show you the past you must understand in order to know the present and the future. Some of these lessons may be very, very difficult for you, so, of course, you can always just say 'no' and I'll leave."

Paul looked around his apartment, scanning the brown carpet, the bookshelves with their pictures of his friends and family, the television and stereo, the five shelves of books. "I think I must be just imagining this," he said, then felt embarrassed and glanced down at his jeans and loafers.

Noah stood up and lifted his left arm, holding his hand flat out about six feet above the floor. Below it the air began to shimmer in a doorway-shaped area. Paul stared in fascination and fear, feeling his heart race. Behind the portal Paul could see a landscape of sand and scrub brush, a distant palm tree, and a sky whose deep blue held a hot and blazing sun.

Noah stepped back and the scene remained. He waved at the portal, and said, "Will you come with me?"

"I've got to get another job," Paul blurted out, immediately realizing how stupid it sounded.

"I'm here to give you a job," Noah said in a calm voice, his hand holding the portal open. "The world is on the brink of disaster, and you are needed."

"Will I come back?"

"Yes," Noah said. "You'll be back here within a few minutes."

"Then why go?"

"Time is relative. We'll be over there for a few hours."

Paul looked around the apartment again, searching for reality anchors; looked out the window and up Eighth Avenue to the buildings, cars, and people hurrying from normal place to normal place in an entirely normal world. He looked at the perfectly normal clock on the wall, which said it was a normal time in the early evening, 5:25. And he looked at the portal.

## Chapter Three

# Manmade Gods

The doorway into another world stood open, shimmering and noiseless, the ghost of Noah standing next to it, his eyes unblinking, his eyebrows knitted together, his lips a thin slit. Was the look anger, or judgement, or hope, or some unfathomable emotion? Paul couldn't guess, and he looked again at the portal, at the world beyond, which stretched off farther into vision than the buildings he could see outside his own living-room window.

"Are you coming with me?" Noah said. His tone of voice implied to Paul that to do otherwise would be a terrible mistake.

"Ok," Paul said, making a decision one part of him feared he may regret, but other parts knew intuitively was the right choice. At the very worse, it would make a heck of a story. His mind was dizzy, but his stomach was now calm, his heart certain, and he felt the muscles of his arms and hands and shoulders relax as the choice was made. He stood up.

Noah stepped through the portal, walked a few paces on the sand in the world beyond the doorway, stopped, turned around and gestured with his hand for Paul to follow him. Paul walked through the portal, noticing as he did that his ears were filled for a moment with a sizzling sound. He stepped onto the sand and was surprised to feel it totally solid and substantial. As he walked to where Noah stood, he looked past him at the desert, stretching from horizon to horizon, the sky so huge and deep and blue it seemed to echo with depth and vastness.

The air smelled fresh, the bright metallic taste of clean oxygen, tinged slightly with a note of distant wood-fires and a spice Paul couldn't identify. The dryness of it cut the back of his nose and throat, and for a moment his eyes watered from the sudden change in humidity and light. The sun hit him with a palpable intensity, and he knew that if he didn't find shade soon his skin would be burned. All around him was rock, sand, and scrub brush, an occasional tree that resembled the mesquite he'd seen in Arizona. On the far horizon he could make out the silhouette of what looked like several men leading heavily laden camels along a distant trail, and on the far horizon to his right what seemed like the beginning of a vast forest. In the distance to his left, he could see the shimmer of water in what looked like irrigation canals, and green fields filled with people tending whatever was growing there. He turned around, and saw through the portal his apartment in New York, and then with a slow fade the portal became fainter and fainter until it vanished, causing Paul's heart to skip a beat.

"How will we get back?" Paul said, trying to control the panic he could hear in his own voice.

"When we need the door, I can re-open it," Noah said.

Paul relaxed, believing him. He said: "Where are we?" Beyond the empty space where the portal had been, Paul could see a walled city of wood and stone buildings, bustling with activity, the center of the city occupied by a square fortress of tall wooden poles, over the top of which peeked a massive stone building. Men stood atop the city's walls, idly carrying bows over their shoulders and spears in their hands.

"This is the city of Nippur," Noah said. "On the other side of the city is a large canal bringing water from the Euphrates River to our west, and in the distance to our south is the city of Ur. To the northwest is Babylon. To the east, near the Caspian Sea, is the land of Nod, where the Bible says Cain went to find his wife."

"But that means there were other people besides Adam and Eve," Paul said.

"Of course there were," Noah said. "The story of Adam and Eve is not the creation story of all humans, it's the creation story of one particular tribe. Every tribe on earth has its own creation story, and every story is about the creation of *their* particular tribe, whether they came from the sun or were born from a god or fell as fruit from a tree or whatever."

"I'd never thought of it that way," Paul said. "But it makes sense, since the Bible says Adam and Eve started out around six thousand years ago, and archeologists tell us humans have been around for two hundred thousand years. It must have been the story of the origin of the tribe we now call the Jews or Hebrews."

Noah shrugged as if it were self-evident, and continued. "Nod is to our east, and what was once called Eden is to our southwest. This is the land you now refer to as ancient Mesopotamia, a part of ancient Sumeria, in your time part of Iraq. It is now, at this moment as we stand here, a thousand years after the floods forced these people upland from where the Tigris and Euphrates rivers once met, and five hundred years after the invasion by the Kurgans."

"Kurgans?"

"They were a herding people who lived north of here, in the areas around the Caucasus Mountains. When the climate changed and floods struck here, at the same time drought hit the Kurgans. Facing famine, they took up the sword and began to move out of their home-lands, looking for food. They spread here, down into In-dia, east into China, and west and north into Europe. Everywhere they went, they assimilated themselves into the local peoples, as they had no empire of their own. They have become largely invisible even by now, five thousand years before you were born, because they have become these people, and the people of India, and of Asia, and of Europe. There has been a mixing of their languages, their ways, and their gods. They brought the alphabet, and that transformed culture, infected it with new ways. You could say it rewired people's brains, made them more ruthless, literal, abstract, and willing to dominate. The left brain, the male brain, took over, be-cause that's the part of the brain where reading is pro-cessed."

"We're at some turning point in history? In the past?"

"Yes. It's about 3,000 B.C., give or take a century. Five thousand years ago, from when we left your apart-ment."

"Why are we here?" Paul said.

"This is your first lesson in wisdom, to prepare you for the Secret." Noah began a brisk stride toward the city, and Paul ran and stumbled to catch up with him.

They walked in silence; Paul felt intuitively that he shouldn't speak, and Noah didn't initiate a conversa-tion. The air was hot, but Paul noticed it was so dry he wasn't sweating. He unbuttoned the white shirt he was wearing to expose the V-neck T-shirt underneath, keeping his sleeves rolled down to protect his arms from the sun. It took about fifteen minutes to reach the walled city. They entered through a gap in the stone wall protected by soldiers playing a game with dice made of white stones. The soldiers glanced at Noah and Paul with curiosity but didn't say anything.

"This is the Ur gate," Noah said as they walked between tall brick pillars. Around this edge of the city, the homes were small and simple, made of sun-dried brick and wood brought from some distant forest.

People gave Noah and Paul odd looks, but didn't comment on them; Paul could sense fear in the air, and noticed that one of the guards got up and ran off into the city. The man glanced at them with a furtive look; Paul felt a dread, as if the fear in the city were contagious, and knew the man had run off to do or say something that would not be in the best interests of Paul and Noah. Perhaps there was money to be made by telling about the strange visitors. Perhaps he was intending to circle around and rob or assault them.

Paul tried to put the man—the spy, he'd decided—out of his mind as they walked down a dusty street towards the fortress in the city-center. He smelled moisture, saw trees rising above the fortress, and the closer they got to the city-center the thicker the vegetation became.

People moved in and through the city with a sense of purpose, some with long hair, dressed in beautiful robes and striding with an air of dignity, most with short-cropped hair, dressed in rags and pulling carts or carrying loads on their heads, shoulders, or backs. It reminded Paul that the Romans and many slaveholding people before them had marked their slaves by cutting their hair. Ragged children ran and played in the dirt, under the watchful eye of adults, or carried loads of sticks or baskets of what looked to Paul like barley. Paul noticed that he'd seen only men; there were no women out in public.

They passed an empty house, and Noah turned and stepped into it through an open door. Paul followed him, happy for the shade. They walked through a large room, down a short hallway, and into a smaller back room with an open window on one side. On the other outer adobe wall was a small recessed area about two feet square and six inches deep. It was positioned just slightly lower than the window and had the effect of being the center of attention of the room; as you walked in you were facing it directly. In the cutout of the wall sat a five-inch-tall figurine made of a red-brown pottery, a woman with a rounded belly, thick thighs, and large breasts that reached down nearly to her legs.

"The house goddess," Noah said. "Before the Kurgans arrived, these people worshipped female deities in their homes, their fields, their temples, and the forests. They understood that women bring forth life but men cannot; they believed that the greatest gods must be women, because the gods bring forth the crops, rain, and everything else in the world. The Kurgans, however, were a people who had learned to survive by conquering and killing and assimilating themselves among other peoples, so they worship life-taking instead of life-giving gods. Warrior gods. Male gods. And when those male gods gave them victory over every peaceful goddess-worshipping people they confronted, they knew their male gods were the greatest and most powerful. So now most of the people they've had contact with have male gods, or at least male gods have become the highest gods. Still, today many of the peasants of Nippur, Babylon, and most of the world worship female goddesses, although the practice will be eliminated within the next four hundred years."

Paul looked at the strangely formed figure and said, "But it's just a statue."

"No, she is a goddess," Noah said, "at least to the people who lived in this house, and to about half of the other residents of this town."

"A female god?"

"Yes. They talk to her, they bring her offerings, they pray to her for good crops, success in childbirth, and good health. But they know they cannot pray to her for success in war, because women are life-bringers and not life-takers. They don't realize it now, but as their population grows and they resort to war to get more wood, land, and food, they will turn to the male war-gods who will usurp the female gods."

"But it's just clay, isn't it?" Paul said, wondering if he should bow before the statue or genuflect or something.

"No, she's a goddess," Noah said. "Not a statue of a goddess, but a goddess herself. She is Aruru, who, with Enlil was the mother of the first seven human men and women, the creator of Gilgamesh, the goddess who gave birth to this tribe, the Sumerians. Each statue in this town is Aruru, and each is she. Before the Kurgans arrived, she was also in the main temple."

"That doesn't make sense," Paul said, remembering what a Catholic friend had told him when he'd asked why people prayed in front of statues of Mary and others in Catholic churches and why she wore around her neck a little gold figure of Jesus on the cross. "It must be a statue that represents something larger than the statue."

"No," Noah said. "She is a goddess. These people are quite certain about that. She has specific powers and abilities, and when they pray to her it is to her," he pointed at the figurine, "to that piece of clay. They are not praying to anything behind her or other than her."

"But she was made by people!"

Noah tilted his head slightly and said, "And who made people?"

Paul felt a moment of dread, a shaking of reality. "Is she really a goddess? I mean can she make it rain and things like that?"

"No and yes," Noah said. "She is only clay for you and me, but she is something more to these people, and that is real, too."

Paul nodded, confused, wondering what it all meant. He felt vaguely uneasy, remembering the first commandment, which said the god of the Bible was a jealous god, and, *You shall have no other gods before me.* But how could you have other gods if no other gods existed? Why would the Bible's god be jealous of other gods if they didn't exist?

"Is this the Wisdom School?"

"There's no single place that is this Wisdom School," Noah said. "The teaching is both outside and inside you. When you are finished, the teachings of the Wisdom School will be within you, and wherever you are they will be."

A clatter from outside the house caught Paul's attention, and he turned as four soldiers ran into the room, the two in the front holding short iron swords and the two in the rear holding spears. All were muscular dark-haired men, dressed in skirted uniforms made of leather strips adorned with bronze medallions and bits of red cloth. The two men in front made menacing gestures toward Paul, who stepped back and put his hands up.

"Whoa, I'm just a tourist," he said, trying to look friendly and sincere.

The man near Noah waved his sword toward Paul, not to cut but to threaten, and an explosion of guttural syllables came from his mouth.

"He says it is against the law of Enlil to be in this place of blasphemy," said Noah. "The family that lived here refused to destroy their goddess, so they were killed. If we stay, we shall be killed, as well." He waved his hand at Paul. "You now have the ability to speak and understand their language. It will sound to you like they are speaking English, and when you speak English, they will understand you in their tongue."

The soldier glared at Noah and said, "It is forbidden that you come here to worship Aruru. You have committed blasphemy!"

Noah calmly replied, "We are visiting dignitaries from a foreign land, and stopped here because we were curious about the local customs."

The two soldiers in the front shook their heads vigorously in disagreement with Noah, and the two in the rear stood at attention, carefully following the conflict but also clearly subordinates. The first soldier who'd spoken, a huge man with black eyes and curly black hair, muscles like rocks under his skin, glared at Noah, who smiled in response. The man shouted, "You lie!"

Noah leaned forward, raised his fist, and shouted back, "I speak the truth!" He waved at Paul. "And the man with me is Nusku, also known as Paul, who is the former chief-minister of Enlil, and now the chief-minister for Anu. As you know, Anu is very angry with Enlil, and so he has sent Paul to speak with Enlil."

The men stepped back and had a hurried discussion in furtive tones.

Paul said, "Who is Enlil?"

"At this moment," Noah said, "he is the head of the pantheon of gods, the creator of humans and of storms. Within a few decades, however, he will be replaced by Anu, the father of Enmesharra, whom Enlil killed. These men know how angry Anu is with Enlil, and they won't intervene in Enlil's business, because he's notorious for his short temper. For example, the people here believe that Enlil created the great flood, which was survived by only one family in an ark."

"Noah's ark?"

"No, this ark was built by a righteous man named Utnapishtim. But the story is the same."

"These people are Jews?"

"No, this land is what your people would call early Sumeria, and these are Sumerians or pre-Babylonians. The ancestors of the Jews live several hundred miles from here, although the two peoples will collide many, many times."

The lead soldier stepped forward, belligerence etched on his face, his muscles twitching. "This man Paul could not be a representative of Anu. His hair has been cut, the sign he is owned. He is a slave, probably your slave."

"His hair reflects the custom of the aristocracy in Anu's land. Look at his clothes, how elaborate they are. He is, himself, a supernatural being."

"And you?" the soldier said.

"I am his servant."

"Hah!" the man screamed, and drove his sword into Noah's stomach. Paul stared, horrified, as Noah's eyes bulged, his mouth opened in a gasp, and a red stain erupted across his tunic. The soldier stepped back, pulling his sword out of Noah's stomach with a self-satisfied look. His partner kept his sword pointed at Paul's stomach.

Paul trembled, feeling as if he might throw up, his heart racing. The light in the room seemed to brighten, and he could hear the quickening breath of the two soldiers. Noah put his hands over his stomach, as if to hold the contents in, and stepped back, his face pale. He opened his mouth, then closed it, as if he'd thought better of whatever he was going to say.

The soldier near Paul pushed his sword toward Paul, backing him into the wall behind him. The soldier stepped forward, the tip of his sword resting on Paul's stomach. The man said, "Now, you tell the truth. Who are you?" Paul felt his palms moisten, his breath speed up. There was no place to run, no way out of the room except past the four soldiers.

"Noah!" Paul said in a low voice, trying to conceal his panic. "What's happening?" He felt the sharp tip of the soldier's sword push hard against the fabric of his shirt, just short of the pressure necessary to pierce the fabric, skin, and muscle under it.

Noah coughed and took a deep, loud breath, then fell to the floor. He lay without movement or breath, the ground soaking up his blood.

The soldier with his spear to Paul's stomach said again, "Who are you?"

Paul thought of the times that he had faked being the assistant to the senator from New York when he wrote his ill-fated story for the *Tribune. Step into the role,* he remembered. *Become the person you're acting you are.*

He drew himself up straight and tall. "I am Paul, and I am here to see Enlil. I have a question for him, on behalf of Anu."

The man who'd stabbed Noah said, "Prove it."

What would Anu's representative say, Paul wondered. Then it came to him.

"I will prove it to Enlil. You are already in great danger of the wrath of Anu and Enlil because you have killed my companion." He fought the catch in his voice and continued. "If you kill me, an even greater destruction will come upon you and your city."

The soldier with his sword to Paul's stomach tensed his muscles, and Paul knew he was preparing for the killing stab. But the leader, who had stabbed Noah and now had an uncertain look on his face, said to his compatriot, "Stop. He is oddly dressed and his face is hairless. Clearly he is from a foreign land. We'll take him to the priests and let Enlil determine his fate."

Paul felt relief wash over him, but knew he had to stay in his role. "And your fate as well," he added, pleased to see the men wince at his words.

They led him at spear-point through twisting roads and narrow streets, children staring and giggling at Paul's clothing, hair, and clean-shaven face. The short-haired adults mostly averted their gaze, while the long-haired men gave him little attention whatsoever except to nod at the soldiers. They came to a gate in the stockade around the central part of the city, and the leader of the soldiers spoke briefly with the spear-bearing gate guards in hushed tones. They stood back, holding their spears respectfully at side arms, and allowed the five to pass.

Paul walked with his head erect, every bit the messenger of a god, guided by the soldiers toward a massive stone building faced with polished marble and granite and trimmed with carefully hewn logs of cedar. On both sides of the large central entrance men sat on colorful blankets, and a slow but steady stream of longhaired noblemen came up to the blankets. Each placed an offering of food or carved stone or metal, took a small embossed bit of pottery that Paul assumed was a receipt, and then backed away, bowing.

Paul and his guards walked through the portal, to shocked looks from the priests collecting the offerings. One began to protest, but one of the four soldiers ran up and began an animated conversation with him. After a few sentences, the man stopped staring at Paul and instead fell silent, his face to the ground. The soldier rejoined the group.

They walked into a huge room, the walls and ceiling decorated with gold, polished woods, and colorful stone mosaics. The floor was polished and oiled light-gray granite, and the soft murmur of voices echoed through the building. A man in a yellow robe with detailed and intricate embroidery in reds and greens sat on a wooden bench next to a door into the innermost room, and the lead soldier spoke with him briefly. Statues of what looked like dogs were on either end of the bench, carved of stone, each about three feet tall. Smaller dog-statues were scattered around the edges of the room, each painted to look more life-like, with red gums, green eyes, and various spots, stripes, and blotches of ochre, tan, black, and straw-yellow. The priest looked Paul up and down carefully, shivered, and nodded with his head in a gesture Paul took as permission to enter. He followed two soldiers into the next room, the other two staying with the priest who guarded the door.

The ceiling stretched forty feet up, the walls made of large, light-brown stones, decorated with elaborate paintings and drawings of bulls and men, metal figures of birds and dogs, and what looked like maps. One large panel had what looked like hieroglyphs carved into its top, and more recently carved alphabetic letters in vertical rows below. All around the room were dozens of pottery and stone-carved statues of dogs and men, many of the men looking like they were holding their necks in pain. The air smelled of cedar smoke, frankincense, and body odor.

A pyramid-shaped stone structure, which Paul recognized from his history classes in college as being called a ziggurat, rose in the center of the room twenty feet or more. It was made of a yellow stone, finely polished with foot-high and foot-deep steps leading from the wide base to the top, reminding him in structure of the small pyramid north of Cancun, Mexico he'd climbed once on a vacation trip. On the three-foot-square top of it stood a ten-foot-tall stone statue of a man holding a purple fabric robe in one hand; a gleaming gold spear in the other. Wings sprouted from his shoulder blades, reaching two feet out behind his shoulders. Fresh fruit and flowers lay all around the statue's feet.

From the way everybody was acting, Paul guessed the statue was Enlil, and so he nodded toward it in a gesture of respectful familiarity. This was the test, and he knew his life depended on how he played out the next few minutes.

Two men dressed in yellow robes sat on elaborately woven mats of red and yellow and gold, facing the statue of Enlil. Before them were opened scrolls of what looked to Paul like either a thick paper or thin white animal skin, and each had a small cup of black ink and a thin brush next to his respective scroll. Both men had long black hair and beards, their dark skin and black eyes proclaiming their Middle Eastern ancestry, their fingernails painted purple, their fingers covered with rings of silver and gold. One was large and stocky, the other thin with the air of an aesthete.

In a single and smooth gesture, both stood and walked toward Paul and his guards.

The thin man spoke first, addressing himself to the soldier in command. "Who is this man you bring into the most holy sanctuary?"

The guard said, "He says he is Nusku, that he now serves Anu. His companion was belligerent, so I killed him. But this man called on the name of Enlil to decide his fate, so we brought him here."

The man nodded. "A wise choice. He is indeed odd of appearance and dress."

"My thoughts exactly," the soldier said. "These are dangerous times. He may be what he says he is, or he may be a spy."

The stocky priest walked up to Paul, putting his face so close Paul could smell the garlic on his breath. "And who do you say you are?" he said, his voice thick with contempt.

"I am Paul, also known as Nusku, and I bring a question from Anu for Enlil."

"We have had no signs, there has been no prophecy. Enlil has made no mention of such a visit."

Paul shrugged. "I am here. Is that not proof enough?"

The thin priest stepped forward. "No. You are a spy."

The soldiers stepped forward, and Paul felt a spear-point touch his left kidney, another sword-point resting on his neck. He remembered how Noah had shook his fist and it had led to his death, and so put his hands into the pockets of his jeans. There, his left hand encountered the Bic lighter Mack had tossed to him earlier in the day.

"No, I am the representative of a god, and have been given my own powers," Paul said, taking his hands from his pockets slowly, keeping the lighter hidden in his left fist. "I am he who controls the elemental forces."

Both guards laughed and the priests looked baffled.

"Say the word and we will take him outside and kill him," said the larger soldier.

"Or kill him here, if it will please Enlil," added the man whose spear was poking Paul's back.

"May I demonstrate?" Paul said to the thin priest, who he'd decided was the one of the four with the greatest authority.

"Demonstrate what?" the priest said, one eyebrow arched.

"I will illuminate this soldier, if it is your will," Paul said.

The priest glanced to the soldier, who said, "I do not trust him."

"What would you do?" the priest said to Paul.

"It's really very simple," Paul said, slowly bringing his left hand up and around so it was just below the beard of the soldier. He flicked the Bic lighter, and the man's beard burst into flame.

The soldier shrieked and his spear clattered to the floor as he grabbed at his burning beard. He hopped around the room, putting the flames out, making an angry keening sound like a wounded animal.

The other soldier stepped back to the doorway, holding his spear with both hands, his eyes wide. The priests both stepped back a few feet from Paul, but watched him carefully. Their faces danced with curiosity and awe.

"You carry fire in your hand?" the thin and elder priest said as the lead soldier picked back up his sword.

"I will kill him now!" the burned soldier said, but his eyes betrayed a deep fear.

"I carry only my magic talisman, given me by Anu," Paul said, displaying the red Bic lighter. "It controls a wide variety of elemental forces. If you would like, I can demonstrate its power to create an earthquake, or a mighty storm with lightning that strikes men dead."

"That is not necessary," the elder priest said, with a quick nod of assent from his companion. He turned to the soldier. "You may leave, and take your companion with you."

"But they killed my friend," Paul said. Now that he was in control, he felt the anger at their casual murder of Noah fill him. It mingled with his fear that he may never return to his own time and place.

"What was the value of your servant?" the younger priest said. "They shall reimburse you."

Paul waved the Bic at the soldier nearest him, making the man flinch and cringe, and then waved it at the other soldier. "My friend was beyond value, so I curse these men. They shall see their own punishment soon enough."

The two men blanched, aghast and bug-eyed, and then turned and ran from the room as if a lion were chasing them.

"So," the elder priest said, eyeing the Bic possessively. "What is your message for Enlil?"

"It is a question, really," Paul said.

"And that question is?" The two priests were staring curiously at Paul, glancing furtively at his blue jeans, white pinpoint Oxford-cloth cotton shirt, and cordovan penny loafers. He realized that he had not seen a single other person wearing pants or shoes.

Paul took a deep breath. "If a man travels through time, how is he to return to his own time?"

"Travels through time?" said the older priest. "Do you mean how does an old man become young again?"

"No," Paul said. "I mean if I were to travel from this moment back to the days when your fathers' fathers were first born, how would I then return to this moment here-and-now?"

"Such travel is impossible," the stocky priest said. "There is no horse which can travel in such a way."

"Perhaps there is a door through which one can step into another time?" Paul said.

"Then walk back through the doorway," the older priest said.

"But the doorway has closed," Paul said.

"And it was first created or opened by Anu?" the older priest said. "He needs help to find it again?"

"It may have been created by a man," Paul said. "Anu is uncertain."

"So the question," the younger priest said, "is how to move through different lifetimes, and whether this doorway you mention is made by the gods or the men, and where or how to find it. Is that correct?"

"That is correct," Paul said.

"We shall consult Enlil," the older man said. "In the meantime, please refrain from further demonstrations of the power of your talisman."

"I will," Paul said, putting the Bic lighter back into his pocket. "Thank you."

The two men went to their rugs and each opened a small wooden box, removing a pinch of a dried green herb, what looked like oregano to Paul. Each put the herb into his mouth, positioning it between cheek and gums, and stood for a moment as they moistened it with saliva. The thin one took what looked like small bits of amber and walked over to a square brick box built out of the far wall. Looking carefully, Paul could see the slight shimmer of air above it indicating heat; it was the source of the smell of cedar smoke. The priest threw the bits of gum onto the coals, and a cloud of frankincense filled the air. He and his compatriot sniffed deeply of it, holding their heads over the coals.

Slowly, as if in a trance, the two men approached the front of the ziggurat, separated by a space of five feet. Marching to a sound beyond Paul's hearing, they slowly climbed the ziggurat, each man's foot lifting from the stones and landing on the stones at the exact same moment, as if their nervous systems were one. They slowly climbed to the top of the ziggurat where they moved together, holding hands now as they stood before the Sumerian god Enlil. The thin one sang something, and then the stocky one, and the song went back and forth for three or four minutes. They bowed low. Then the thin one said something directly to the face of the statue, using tonality that clearly was questioning.

The two men at the top step of the ziggurat held their posture, as if frozen, for several long minutes. Outside the building, Paul could hear the sound of people talking, of dogs barking, of a baby screaming. The coals sizzled softly. The smell of frankincense tickled his nose and left a thick, bitter taste in the back of his throat.

One of the priests began to nod and make a soft noise through his nose, a grunt of assent. Soon the other man was also nodding and grunting. Both raised their arms, the hands between them still held tightly, and sang a short chant, bowed, and backed slowly down the ziggurat together.

They approached Paul and the thin one, a bit of greenish spittle drooling from the left corner of his mouth into his beard, hummed a soft tune.

Paul hummed back at him, the first few bars of *Row, Row, Row Your Boat.*

The men nodded together, as if Paul had uttered a

profound statement. Their motions seemed oddly slow motion, and Paul wondered if the herb they'd put into their mouths was a psychoactive drug. Frankincense, he remembered from his friends in Catholic school, was also something that, when inhaled in sufficient quantities, could produce a mild high.

"Did you hear the voice of Enlil?" Paul said.

"Yes."

"And it said?"

The old priest spoke with a soft and awe-filled voice. "Enlil said, 'The Creator of the Universe brought forth humans so humans could create the gods.'"

"That's all?"

"We are shocked by this," the young priest said. "It must be transcribed."

"It is a profundity beyond understanding," the thin, elder priest said. "A new revelation. It must contain the answer to your quest. It is the word of Enlil."

## Chapter Four

# The Taste of Salt

Paul sat on the bank of the canal that carried the waters of the Euphrates River into Nippur and its surrounding fields. A hundred yards across, it flowed with a sluggish current, and smelled of vegetation and sewage. The surface was thick with brown scum and green algae, blue and brown water spiders danced across the water's skin, and under the surface Paul could see black beetles swimming with rowing-like motions of long jointed hind legs. The sun was close to the horizon, an ancient reddening disk, and the earth cooling into the empty blue-black sky made Paul feel chilly. Behind them, the city was shifting into evening gear, and the smell of wood smoke drifted out over the windless plains.

He had walked here in silence, after the audience with Enlil and his priests. It was a few hundred feet from where he'd fruitlessly searched for the now-missing portal back to twenty-first century New York. On the way all the soldiers and citizens of Nippur had given him wide berth; apparently word traveled fast here. He'd checked out the empty house, but there was no trace of Noah's body. Only the bloodstained floor gave a clue to the events of the afternoon.

Paul was still trying to understand the words of Enlil. So he wouldn't forget, he took out the little spiral-note-pad from his shirt pocket and wrote, *The Creator of the Universe brought forth humans so humans could create the gods.* He wondered what it meant; it couldn't be a literal truth, but had to be a metaphor for something deeper. And, more important, he wanted to know why this was something new, a revelation, to the two priests. They acted as if they'd actually heard the statue say something new, something they'd never before considered, some-thing radical and startling. A deep and ancient truth, an unknowable paradox. Was it a shared hallucination? The recital of some well-worn teaching and they were only performing in their amazement? And how would it help him get home, in any case?

Paul thought about New York, how far away it was both in time and distance. In a way it was as if it had never existed; in another way it was as if this were all a bizarre dream. He looked over at a swarm of gnats that extended from a foot above the water to about three feet up. There were probably a thousand insects in the egg-shaped airborne community, each flying about as if randomly, few ever breaking the perimeter of the swarm. Each was an individual, yet they moved as one.

*Humans create the gods*, he thought, recalling the man-made statues. Noah had said that the Greeks and Romans would have called him a god. Was it possible?

Paul stood up on the riverbank and turned around to look back to where the portal had once been open. "Noah!" he shouted. "I create you!"

The landscape didn't change.

"I command the portal to open!"

The only motion was the slow, slight movement of a distant man on camelback.

"Now!" he screamed. "Please!"

A voice from behind him said, "Why all the noise?"

Paul spun around, and Noah was sitting on the riverbank next to where Paul had been sitting moments earlier.

"Noah! You're back!"

"I was never gone," Noah said, gesturing to Paul to sit back down.

"But I created you," Paul said, sitting cross-legged next to Noah. "Just now. I willed you into existence, just like Enlil said I could."

Noah chuckled. "I'm sorry, Paul, but it's not quite that simple. You still have much to learn."

"But you're here!"

"I've always been here. You just didn't see me."

"You mean you didn't die on the floor?"

"No," Noah said. "Of course not. But I sure put on a good show, didn't I?" His eyes crinkled into a broad smile. "Those guys are still looking for my body so they can give it a proper burial. They're convinced that maybe, if they throw enough goodies into my casket, it'll reverse the curse of your Bic lighter." He chuckled. "Five thousand years from now somebody will find a hieroglyph about it. It'll hopelessly confuse the archeologists of the twenty-first century."

"Do you mean that what Enlil said was wrong?" Paul said.

"No, but it wasn't entirely right, either. It was an understanding expressed in the way people of this time can comprehend."

"Well, I'm supposedly five thousand years more advanced than these folks, and I'm confused by it. What did it mean?"

Noah ran the fingers of his left hand, the skin leathery and cracking, through his beard, then pointed to the canal. "Where did this water come from?"

"You said the Euphrates River."

"And where did the water in the Euphrates come from?"

Paul thought for a moment, then said, "Runoff from rains, collecting in small streams and springs?"

"And where did that water come from?"

"The sky, as rain."

"And where did that water come from?"

"Evaporation."

"Evaporation from what?"

"Well, four-fifths of the world is ocean, so I'd guess that while some of it came as evaporation from land, most of it was evaporation from the oceans."

"So," Noah said, lifting a finger into the air. "We could say that the water in that canal in front of us came from the ocean?"

"Sure," said Paul. "And it's going back to the ocean, too, eventually."

Noah nodded. "And if I were to get a cup of that water, or any water, and proclaim it to be the ocean, what would you say?"

Paul laughed. "I'd say you were wrong!"

"But it's part of the ocean."

"Yes, but it's not the ocean itself."

Noah nodded again, and ran his right hand over his beard, pulling it together in his hand, as if to nod his head with his hand via his beard. "Yes."

"Are you saying that all of these gods are just bits of a larger god, the way this water is a bit of the larger ocean?"

"No," said Noah emphatically. "What I'm speaking about is what people call things, not what they are."

"I'm lost," said Paul.

"I can call my cup of water the ocean, and may even be able to convince some people it is. Particularly those who have never seen the ocean. Right?"

"Probably."

"But it's not the ocean."

"Nope."

"Yet a thousand different peoples are all pointing to their particular gods and saying, 'These ones are the ocean!' Or, 'This one is the only ocean and all the other oceans don't exist.'"

"But there is only one God," Paul said.

Noah nodded and pulled his eyebrows together, his nose flared momentarily. "Tell me about this One God."

Paul looked at the water, picked a piece of grass from beside him, and began to tear it lengthwise. "He's a jealous god."

"And this god's name is?"

"Jehovah, I think."

"But the scriptures say that His Name cannot be pronounced. There are only the four consonants, but no vowels. Nobody knows how to say the Name."

"Ok, so we don't know His Name," Paul said, rubbing the side of his hand where he scratched it pushing the little girl out of the way of the truck.

"You know what the One God said when Moses said, 'Who are you?'"

"Something like, 'I am me'?"

"He said, 'I am that I am.' In other words, 'You can't know who I am.'"

"Why not?"

"Can a cup hold—and thus understand—the ocean?"

Paul looked at the sun, now a deep crimson, halfway below the horizon as shadows stretched and moved across the land. "I get it," he said, feeling for the first time an understanding and identity with the God of his childhood, the God of the Bible.

"And what does He look like?" Noah said.

Paul rolled up one of the scraps of leaf and dropped it on the ground in front of him. "A burning bush?"

"Actually, the message Moses got was that nobody could look at Him and live."

"That's pretty drastic."

"If you interpret it literally. Again, though, I'd say that the message was, 'I cannot be fully seen with your senses, nor described with your words, so don't even bother to try.'"

"Like radio waves," Paul said, the insights piling one atop another, his heart racing as he saw how it all fit together, clearly heard the message, felt the reality of it.

"What do radio waves have to do with it?" Noah said.

"Well, radio waves have been around forever. Neutron stars emit them, for example. They've always been here. But we don't have sense organs for them, so to us they seem not to exist. If you tried to tell the people of Nippur that with a small box in the palm of my hand I could pull out of the air the voice of somebody thousands of miles away, they'd say that I was crazy. If I did it, they'd say I was divine or a wizard. It wasn't until radio receivers were invented that we realized there was something there. The radio waves. So we have no receiver for God."

Noah pulled on a bit of his hair that fell over his left shoulder. "I wouldn't make that assumption yet. Which was invented first, the radio receiver or the transmitter?"

"Geez, I have no idea," Paul said. "Assuming you mean the man-made transmitter. That's an interesting question."

"So how could we summarize what you now understand and know?" Noah said.

Paul thought back on Enlil, on the goddess in the house, on what he'd read in the Bible, on his own experiences of *knowing* God was real but being totally incapable of describing that knowing. "I'd guess that it would be something like, 'Anytime you try to describe God, you miss Him.'"

"Him?"

"Or Her?"

"Actually, both are 'descriptions.'"

"Ah, yes!" Paul said, pulling his notepad and pen out of his pocket. "But most languages require a gender for pronouns. And the description of God we most often use came out of a male-dominated culture."

"Does that mean God is a male, or a female?" Noah said.

"I'd guess neither. God is beyond gender. Or do gods each have different genders?"

"Only gods like Enlil," Noah said. "Otherwise, it's 'I am that I am.' So you could say, 'Any god you can describe is not the Creator of the Universe, because the Creator of the Universe is bigger and vaster than anything that can be described by humans.'"

Paul nodded and scribbled in his pad, *Any god you can describe is not the Creator of the Universe, because the Creator of the Universe is bigger and vaster than anything that can be described by humans.* "I can understand that. And it's getting dark and I'm getting cold."

Noah clapped his hands, and they were sitting back on the two sofas in Paul's living room in New York City.

## Chapter Five

# Even the Dogs?

"Hey, how'd you do that?" Paul demanded, picking up the wineglass he'd left on the coffee table. He took a sip and the familiar tang made him salivate, the moisture fulfilling the deep thirst he'd developed in his hours in the desert. The familiar sun outside was setting beyond sight of Manhattan's buildings and the familiar clock said it was 5:36. They'd been gone eleven minutes, if that, and Paul realized how important *familiar* and *normal* were to him.

"You mean the hand-clap?" Noah said.

"Yeah, what happened to the portal?"

Noah stood up, brushed himself off, and said, "It's the old Star Trek thing. I've gotta do it for people of your generation."

"Star Trek?"

"Yep. You expected to see a portal or doorway to

73

some other dimension, right? I gave you one. Plus I wanted something that included the ability for you to choose to go or not go, and that worked as well as anything."

"You didn't need the portal?"

Noah walked out to the kitchen, vanishing in the ordinary way beyond the wall between the living room and kitchen. "I don't even need this body," his voice said as Paul heard the refrigerator door open.

Noah returned with a glass of milk in his hand. "If you were an Apache, I'd have appeared as somebody totally different." He put the glass of milk down on the coffee table, and so fast that it appeared visually seamless to Paul, Noah changed into a large yellow-brown dog. "This is Coyote," the dog said, reaching over to drop its long red tongue into the glass of milk. It made a messy slurp that splashed milk on the side of the glass and the tabletop. "Oops," it said, licking up the milk from the glass tabletop.

There was a fast rap on the apartment door, and Paul jerked up, alert. The rap repeated, and Paul recognized it as the signature of Rich, from next door. He looked at the coyote, then the door, then back at the coyote. It sneezed, and before the sneeze was finished the coyote had vanished and Noah stood before Paul, this time dressed in a brown tweed jacket with leather elbow patches, dark brown wool slacks, and battered

Hush-Puppies shoes. He held an unlit meerschaum pipe in his right hand; his hair and beard were neatly trimmed, and he looked every bit the role of a professor from the nineteenth century.

Paul felt his muscles tense, as the image of the street preacher telling him he'd burn in hell sprang to mind, unbidden. "This is truly weird," he said. "Are you some kind of demon?"

"A matter of definitions," Noah said, as Rich rapped on the door again. "Can you imagine how your Christian or Muslim or Jewish priest would react if I appeared to him as a talking coyote? To him, no matter what I said or did, I'd be a bad god or under-god. They all have a very specific definition of a very human-like god, and of the good guys who hang out with Him, and they all know that once the era of the institutional church began, the era of the supernatural ended."

"You rather contradict that," Paul said, stepping back towards the door.

"Yes. As soon as you try to define the Creator of the Universe, you have missed, like trying to catch radio waves in your hands. When St. Francis met me, he knew I was his friend, that I am working on behalf of the Creator of the Universe and on behalf of humanity. So did Brother Lawrence, and Meister Eckhard, and Saint John of the Cross. A televangelist, of course, would only think well of me if I gave him a big donation." Noah looked at his pipe and laughed. "Answer the door. I'm acceptable now."

Paul watched him, wild and conflicting emotions rushing through him. Seeing the talking coyote had shocked him so deeply he was wondering if he should grab Rich at the door and run out of the apartment. Noah saw the expression on his face and smiled in a friendly, reassuring way.

Paul walked to the door and opened it: Rich was standing there, wearing black slacks and an expensive yellow silk shirt. "I just talked with Bob . . ." he paused in mid-sentence as he glanced past Paul and saw Noah. "Who's the old guy?"

"Just a friend," Paul said, standing in the doorway so Rich wouldn't just walk in, as was his usual habit. He always expected Paul to wait to be invited into his apartment, but always just walked right into Paul's, as if he knew he was part of the aristocracy and Paul wasn't.

"Hello," Noah said in a loud voice from the living room.

Rich pushed past Paul and walked over to Noah, his hand outstretched. Paul closed the door, feeling offended by Rich's habit of seeing every human in the world as a potential contact who may someday, somehow need a lawyer.

"Pleased to meet you," Rich said to Noah, holding

out his hand. "I'm Rich Whitehead, the attorney. Just dropped by with a job offer for Paul."

"Pleased to meet you," Noah said.

"And you are?" Rich said, letting the last word hang.

"You may call me 'Professor.'"

"Professor? Professor who? And of what?"

Noah looked out the window for a moment, as if he were searching for an answer, then said, "Faust. Ethics."

Rich laughed. "That's a good one," he said, but then caught himself when he saw that Noah wasn't laughing with him. "You serious?"

Noah replied in a slow, serious voice. "You're a lawyer. Didn't you learn about me when you undertook your profession?"

Rich smiled. "I get it now. Paul told you about me being a lawyer . . ."

"No, you did. Are you here to sell your soul? If so, I'll have to call somebody else, as I work on, as they say, the good side of the street."

Rich turned to Paul and pointed a thumb at Noah. "He's great, you know that? Really great."

"Yeah, great," Paul said, wondering how Rich would have reacted to the coyote, wondering what he'd say if Paul even tried to tell him about the events of the past hours . . . or minutes, depending on which world you were referring to.

"Listen," Rich said, "I'm on my way out with Cheryl,

and then I've gotta head back to the firm. But I called Bob Harrell, he's my boss, and he said that as a matter of fact they could use a good writer, if you're willing to work free-lance. Probably twenty or thirty hours a week, and they'll only pay forty dollars an hour, but it's a start."

Elation and relief filled Paul. "Forty dollars an hour! That's more than what I was making at the *Tribune*!"

"Yeah, well, now you know where the money is," Rich said, his tone implying that he'd just thrown a bone to a mongrel. He reached into his back pocket, pulled out a card, turned and handed it to Noah, saying, "If you ever need a good law firm, we do everything."

Noah took the card with his right hand, holding it with the pipe, and looked it over. With his left hand, he reached into the pocket of his white shirt and pulled out a business card, which he handed to Rich. "And if you ever decide you want to forsake evil for good, give me a call."

Rich gave him a smug expression as he took the card, which, as he touched it, burst into a flash of blue flame. "Hey!" he yelled, jerking his hand back and sprinkling a bit of black ash.

"Apparently you're not pure enough to touch my card," Noah said in a dry tone.

"That's not funny! You could have burned me!"

Noah nodded. "And then you'd sue me?"

Rich's eyes narrowed. "Damn right."

"Americans pray to their doctors, 'Save my life, good sir.' The new high priests of life. But they live in fear of their lawyers. 'Please don't destroy me, sir, or take my home.' You are one of the modern-day demons."

"Careful," Rich said. "The law is an honorable profession."

"Have you ever helped the poor?" Noah said. His tone of voice trembled with a very Noah-like righteousness that caused Paul to hold his breath.

"No," Rich sneered. "They want help, they can go to law school like I did."

"Got it all figured out, don't you?" Noah said.

"Are you trying to say something?"

"Sir," Noah said, his voice a whisper, "are you interested in riches and power?"

Rich glanced at Paul as if to ask if he was being ridiculed. Paul let his breath out and shrugged, wishing Rich would drop it and leave.

"Yeah, of course," Rich said, using his how-dare-you lawyer tone. "Who isn't?"

"Then there is somebody waiting for a discussion with you," Noah said. He put Rich's card in his pocket, the pipe in his mouth, and turned around to look out the window.

Rich stood for a moment, dismissed, then walked past Paul toward the door. "Weird friend you've got there," he said as he stepped into the hall and pulled the door closed.

Paul turned and Noah was back to his former appearance of long hair, beard, and white tunic.

"I don't know what to make of all this," Paul said.

"Maybe I shouldn't have shape-shifted," Noah said. "I didn't mean to startle you. I apologize for not staying within your belief structure."

"It was pretty weird," Paul said, some of his composure returning.

"And it is true that if you were an Apache, that would have certified me as a 'real spirit.' Although the Coyote doesn't always have the best of reputations, and I suppose, in retrospect, college professors aren't much better." He chuckled to himself. "I could be a bear . . ."

"Don't," Paul interjected.

"Just an idle thought," Noah said. "But the important point is that it all illustrates the final teaching I am here to give you from those many of the Wisdom School."

"Which is?"

"Do you have a remote control for that TV?" Noah said.

"That doesn't sound like a 'teaching' to me," Paul said, glancing at the remote control on the end table between him and the closet near the front door.

Noah nodded at the remote control and said, "Toss it to me."

Paul reached over, picked it up, and handed it to Noah, who pointed it at the TV and pushed the Power button. The TV sprang to life, two big-haired women punching each other while a guy waving a folding chair tried to hit them both.

"Right now," Noah said, "for that TV set, the only show that exists in the known universe is this program, right?"

"I suppose you could say that," Paul said.

"Do you see anything else?"

"No, but you're the one with the remote control. And there are some TVs where you can pop another channel into a little window in the corner."

"You know what I mean. We're tuned to this frequency and it seems like it's the only thing that exists. If you were to give this TV to somebody from a tribe in Borneo, and not give them the remote control and throw away the channel-changing knob, all they'd ever know existed is this one channel. You understand?"

"Yes," said Paul, taking a drink of his wine and wondering where Noah was going with the TV metaphor.

"So the Creator of the Universe made the creation out of what?"

"Hydrogen?" Paul was baffled by the sudden change of direction of the questions.

"That's the smallest element, the smallest atom. But it's made out of what?"

"Electrons, neutrons, and protons."

"And they're made of?"

"I dunno. Subatomic particles of some sort. Quarks and mesons and stuff like that."

"And they're made of?"

"I wasn't a physics major," Paul said. "I stuck with journalism."

Noah nodded. "Which is part of why I'm here, so you can write this story. But back to the question. The smallest known particles exhibit properties of both matter *and* energy. In other words, all matter is made of energy. The amount of energy it took to make, for example, this remote control, is equal to the mass of the remote control times about thirty-five billion, which is the speed of light squared. E equals MC squared. And if you were to convert the matter in this remote control back into the energy it's made of, the amount of energy that would be released would be about thirty-five billion times its mass. Atomic bombs and all that."

"I remember this stuff now from high school," Paul said. "Seems a little odd that Noah would be lecturing me about physics."

Noah snorted. "Boat-builders have historically been at the forefront of science. Out of necessity. I knew geometry and trigonometry before they were named."

"So you learned physics?"

"Actually, I can know anything that is known. And so can you."

"Huh?"

"Just trust me on that one. One day it will be part of your experience." He stood up and walked over to the television. "So, back to TV and physics. The universe is made up of a seamless spectrum of energy, from the most subtle to the most coarse, and of matter which floats in that energy the way ice cubes float in a bucket of water. You with me?"

"Sure," Paul said, taking another drink of the Chardonnay.

"Maybe you shouldn't drink too much of that wine," Noah said. "I remember when Paul told Timothy to quit drinking water and stick to wine, but it's not generally good advice, particularly if you're trying to learn something that'll help you save the world."

Paul put the glass down on the table, thinking that he didn't want to offend anybody who could travel through time and turn himself into a coyote. "Whatever you say."

Noah lifted one eyebrow and looked for a moment like he was going to say something, but then turned back to the TV. "Ok, so we have these women who are fighting. Well, now it's a woman and some guy wearing a dress fighting. Anyhow, we have this station. You with me?"

"Yeah."

"Let's say that this TV station represents part of the spectrum of energy."

"Ok."

"Which it really, in fact, does. It has a specific frequency, like 174 Megahertz. Each TV station has a different channel, or frequency; each is at a different vibrational rate. Each is a different energy."

"Right."

"Similarly, we can detect certain frequencies with our senses. We can see visible light, we can feel heat, and we can hear vibrations in the air from about 40 to about 17,000 vibrations per second, which we call sound. Any others you know of?"

Paul thought for a moment, and said, "Taste and smell?"

"Actually, in those cases you're analyzing the molecular structure of matter. Your taste buds and nose are little chemical detectors."

"So what else is there? That's sight, sound, and touch. We only have five senses."

"There's one more sense that any doctor can tell you about, but most people overlook. It's in your inner ear, called the cochlea, and is a gravimeter. It measures a form of energy called gravity."

"Our sense of balance?"

"Right. It's what allows you to sit up straight now

without falling over. Assuming you haven't had too much wine." Noah smiled at his own joke.

"And I haven't," Paul said, thinking that he rather liked this guy. Noah had saved his life and shown him the past, and was now trying to teach him something that seemed very odd but must be critically important if it was the information that could save the world.

"So you can tune into a few channels. Let's say, for convenience sake, four. Light, heat, sound, and gravity. Everybody knows about those, and everybody agrees on them. So it's like you have a TV with only four channels on its selector knob, even though the cable company has two hundred channels available."

The picture of a coyote telling him these things popped into Paul's mind for a moment, and he shook it out before he started laughing. "Ok, go on," he said.

Noah tilted his head to one side. "You okay?"

"Yeah. I'm with you."

"Okay," Noah said, waving the remote control at the TV like it was a magic wand. "So there are only a few channels you can receive, but there are many out there, because we know that the spectrum of energy is vast and seamless. So you only know a tiny bit of reality. Did you know, by the way, that dogs actually see smells?"

"No," said Paul, hoping Noah wasn't going to pop into being a coyote again.

"Seriously," Noah said. "When it happens in humans, it's called synesthesia, and considered a brain disease. People who see sound or taste colors. But with dogs, much of the visual part of the brain is used to process information from the nose. Dogs actually see smells. They create smell maps in their minds, and a blind dog can function almost as well as a sighted dog as long as there's a scent trail for him to follow."

"Another channel?"

"More or less. Pardon the digression. I rather like dogs."

"I can understand why."

Noah nodded as if it was a perfectly normal conversation, to talk about being a dog and the nature of reality, and said, "Ok, so we have these two facts in summary. One is that everything in creation is made out of energy. Everything originated from a single energy, the subtlest energy, and as that energy became more and more coarse, it diversified and came into being as X-rays and light and gravity and sound and the whole thing. Then it congealed into matter and the physical universe banged into existence. This is the creation story as told by both physics and Genesis and John. First there was God, then God made light. Or, 'In the beginning was the Word.' You understand?"

"I think so," Paul said. "First there was the most subtle energy, the finest energy, and it slowed down and became coarser and coarser, making all the energies we can detect, and then some of it slowed down even more—the way slowed-down or cooled-down liquid water becomes solid ice. Thus it became matter, and the energy and matter together are what we call the physical universe."

"Right," said Noah. "Exactly right. And so this then raises two questions: one, what *was* that First Energy that everything else was made from; and, two, is it possible that we can detect that First Energy with our nervous systems? Is it one of the 'channels' we can receive?" He hit the power button on the remote control, and the screen of the TV turned black. He pointed the remote control at Paul, as if it could bring the answer from him.

Paul looked at the remote control pointed at him, and felt his mind go fuzzy. What was the first energy? X-rays? Gamma rays? They're all things that are easily detected by machines: they couldn't be the most subtle, most original energy in the universe . . .

"Here's a clue," Noah said. "If you could detect that First Energy, you'd discover that at that level, the entire physical universe is solid. It's *all* made of that stuff, even the apparently empty spaces between things, because the empty space is part of the Creation, too."

Paul nearly jumped off his chair. "It's God!"

"Right!" Noah said. "Or, more correctly, it's The Creator of the Universe. You folks have so badly munged up the word 'God' with your televangelists and all. It's important to differentiate between Everything That Is and some old man with a beard and a big stick who goes after people who join the wrong church or don't send in enough money."

"But what about those people who see God as an old man on a throne? Is He real?"

"Of course He is, if they believe," Noah said. "And there can be great power in such total belief, although if it's lived without a larger understanding it can lead to problems like religious wars. You'll learn more about that from your next teacher."

"Wow," Paul said, feeling a sudden breathlessness, the same he'd felt years ago as a child when he'd gone to Midnight Mass with a friend and heard Handel's *Messiah.* He looked around the room for a moment, thinking *everything I'm looking at is made of and by God!*

"Do you think you can detect this most subtle energy with your human—or even a mammalian—nervous system?"

"I don't know," said Paul, but as he spoke the words he had an intuition that he *could* detect the presence of God. He'd done it, and he knew it. That Midnight Mass. Looking out an airplane window on his first trip in a jet. When he'd fallen in love with Wendy when he was sixteen . . . "Love!" he said, interrupting his own train of thought.

"Wonderful!" Noah said, tossing the remote control onto the couch where he'd been sitting. "Even the teachings which will help you understand the Secret are not secrets, as you now see, hear, and feel. People mouth them all the time, yet they fail to *know* them, to live them. You'll find this, for example, verbatim in the Bible at the end of one John four. You'll find it again in a hundred other places, including Deuteronomy six, at the beginning of the Gospel of John, and in the sacred writings of virtually every religion of the world." He pointed his finger at Paul. "You have begun a work, the work of saving the world, from which you can never turn back."

"I know that, now," Paul said.

"So it's time for me to go, as you have other lessons to learn from other teachers and I have other work to do at this critical time on the Earth."

"Not yet . . ."

"I must," Noah said with a broad, loving smile. "But don't think it hasn't been fun."

And Noah vanished.

Paul jumped up, ready for another apparition, or a coyote to run from the kitchen, or a voice to begin talking from the ceiling, but nothing happened. The room was empty. He knew, somehow, that Noah had left and he was alone.

"Hello?" he said, but the only answer was the sound of a siren down on Eighth Avenue. "Noah?" There was no reply.

He stood up and walked through the apartment; the kitchen, the bathroom, the bedroom, but it was empty. He opened the door into the hallway, but there was nothing but light-blue linoleum and off-yellow walls lit by a fluorescent bulb in the ceiling.

Paul closed the door and walked over to the bookshelf, which he scanned for a moment with a growing feeling of excitement and anticipation. He'd had the book his entire life, the wisdom in his hand, and never understood it.

He pulled his mother's Bible off the top shelf, thinking about love. Turning it to the Book of Deuteronomy, where the Ten Commandments were given, he read: *And thou shalt love the LORD thy God with all thine heart, and with all thy soul, and with all thy might.*

He flipped the pages to the Gospel of John, and read: *In the beginning was the Word, and the Word was with God, and the Word was God. The same was in the beginning with God. All things were made by him; and without him was not any thing made that was made.*

Could it be? Paul wondered. Right in front of me all the time? That the universe was created by an energy that humans have since called God? That everything, from the stars to the taxis to the dog on the street is made of that same stuff? And we've named that energy, just as we named 2000 cycles-per-second "sound," or a few trillion cycles-per-second "light." But the name we've given that energy, the presence of our Creator, when we feel it in the normal course of life is "love," and built into our nervous systems is the ability to detect it, to know it?

With trembling hands, he turned to the fourth chapter of First John, and read: *Beloved, let us love one another: for love is of God; and every one that loveth is born of God, and knoweth God. He that loveth not knoweth not God; for God is love.*

He read it again and whispered softly, "So it is true. They've been trying to tell me for two thousand years." Slowly Paul put the Bible back, walked to the sofa, and sat down. He leaned forward, put his face in his hands, feeling an incredible loss for all the wasted, frightened years. "We all had it wrong all along," he said aloud. He knew it was a breakthrough, a total change in his life, a completely new understanding.

He took out his notepad and wrote, *The energy we call love is the most pure and delicate and powerful way our nervous systems, our minds, can touch the mind of God. It's how we know God, for God is love.* He'd have to share it with others. It could change the world!

And he knew it was only the beginning of his schooling in the Mysteries.

## Chapter Six

# Eggs and Tabasco

Paul Abler awoke the next morning from a wild kaleidoscope of dreams. Most were of visits to ancient times and places; to Sumeria and Palestine, to Nippur and Jerusalem, to the priests of Enlil, and to Jesus wandering with a small band of men and women across the remote deserts of the Galilee. In each place Paul had been given some great Truth, a great knowledge, which he had to take to the people of the twenty-first century, lest all die in a massive, self-created disaster. Yet, awakening, he couldn't remember the details of any of the Truths, except what he'd learned the afternoon before from Noah and written in his notepad.

Wan morning light filled his bedroom, illuminating the pile of books he'd brought home the night before. They were the result of his spending hours in four different bookstores, finding and buying the sacred texts and commentaries of Islam, Hinduism, Buddhism, Judaism, and Christianity, as well as everything he could find on shapeshifters, angels, and Noah. He'd fallen asleep, around two in the morning, with *The Practice of the Presence of God*, by the seventeenth century Carmelite monk and dishwasher Brother Lawrence, on his chest. Only total fatigue and exhaustion tore him from it and threw him into the world of sleep.

The clock beside him said it was twenty-five minutes after six, and the rapidly brightening sunlight told him the cold gray clouds of the day before had dispersed and this would be a sunny February morning. He climbed out of bed and headed for the bathroom, wearing only his Jockey shorts, when the phone rang.

He detoured to the kitchen and picked up the wireless phone from its cradle on the wall. "Hello?"

"Paul, what the hell are you two trying to do to me?!" shrieked a familiar-sounding voice.

"What?" Paul said. "Who . . ."

"This is Rich! It's happened three times now! Twice last night when I was alone in elevators, and then this morning in my bathroom. Call him off or I'll have both your butts in jail this afternoon!"

"What are you talking about?"

"The devil!"

"What?"

"You know!" Rich screamed over the phone. "Red

coat, red skin, goatee, horns, pitchfork, smells like sulfur. You know what I'm talking about!"

"You saw the devil?"

"Saw? *Saw*? He keeps asking if I'm ready to sign the contract!"

"What contract?"

"Don't give me that. This has gone too far. The first time, maybe, that was funny. But this is too much. You call him off, or, so help me, Paul, I'll turn your life into a hell you can't imagine. You'll never get another job, you'll never get credit, and you'll never find a landlord east of China who'll rent you an apartment! Do you hear me?"

"Rich, calm down . . ."

"Whadaya mean, calm down! You got some weird guy doing parlor tricks in your apartment, and he makes some idiotic remark to me, and now he's following me around throwing holograms or some kind of illusion at me." He paused for a moment, as if a thought had occurred to him, then continued, "Or he gave me some kind of a drug. I'll bet that's it. I'll bet it was in that business card, in the paper, and when it burned up I smelled the smoke and that's how it got into me, or it was on the paper and went through my skin and he burned the paper to destroy the evidence. He had to know what kind of drug it was, because he implied what kind of hallucination I'd have. I tell you, pal, this is one trip I'm never gonna forget, and neither are you!"

"Rich, I really don't have any idea what you're talking about . . ."

"Bull!" Rich snorted. "You probably think this is funny; old Rich, a big-shot lawyer, squirming and freaked out. Maybe you're even gonna write it up, it'll be your big story to sell to some paper. Make you the famous reporter again. Well, I'll show you squirming and freaked out, buddy! I'm on the board of directors of this building, and you're out of here. Do you understand? Out of here!"

There was the abrupt sound of Rich's phone being slammed down, and then Paul heard only the dial tone. "Twice in two days," he said to himself as he pushed the button to hang up the phone, walking toward the bathroom and shower that he hoped would make him feel like today was a fresh start. As he walked by the living room, he glanced at the sofa where Noah had sat, and wondered who or what the next angel—he much preferred the word to "ghost"—would be, do, and say. If another angel came at all.

Seven-thirty, an hour later, Paul walked into the Fashion Coffee Shop at the corner of Eighth Avenue and 27th Street. The restaurant was standard New York issue, with Formica-topped tables, metal and plastic chairs, good food, and a kitchen staff who worked with the cheerfulness and speed that their heavily accented English proved was immigrant-working-to-make-it-in-the-big-city.

Mary was waiting on tables and Paul was pleased to see her familiar face. A twenty-one year old psychology student at Hunter College on Manhattan's East Side, she usually worked the breakfast/lunch shift that coincided with the once-a-week breakfasts Paul had treated himself to over the past six months.

In little bits and pieces he'd learned that she had a small apartment a few blocks off Central Park, paid for by her parents, and she worked to cover all her other non-tuition and non-rent expenses. She didn't have a current boyfriend both because of her notions about chastity—not shared by most of the men who'd expressed an interest in dating her—and her desire to get through college before making "any permanent plans." The top of her head came up to Paul's eyes, and she had a pleasant figure that skirted the edge of tomboy. Long chestnut hair cascaded down her back, gathered into a ponytail by a pink Scrunche, and her blue-gray eyes often seemed to be looking into some deep place within Paul when she listened to him talk about himself or his goals as a reporter.

They'd been friendly and flirtatious with each other for the past few months, although Paul had been keeping his reserve, as he'd felt there had been some sort of a commitment in his relationship with Susan.

"How ya doin', Paul?" Mary said as he headed for the table he liked by the front window.

"Fine," he said. "How're you, Mary?"

She walked past him, close enough he could smell her perfume, a faint flowery musk, and she said, "I'm great. But I'll get better." She winked, grinned, and continued on over to the coffee maker.

As he sat down, feeling pleasantly warmed by her presence, she put a cup of black coffee in front of him and said, "Lessee. I'll bet you'd like a Greek omelet, whole wheat toast, home fries with onions, and Tabasco?"

He smiled at her, noticing the twinkle in her blue-gray eyes, and said, "Exactly."

"Even though you had the same thing yesterday?" She scrunched up her face as if she'd just noticed something important. "This is the first time in six months you've been in here twice in a week. Normally it's every Thursday morning, just like clockwork, but here you are on Friday morning, too."

"I decided to treat myself twice," Paul said. "Couldn't stay away from your smile."

She beamed, spun around with an exaggerated gesture as if she were a ballerina, and headed back toward the kitchen, humming along with the music the cooks were listening to on the radio.

Paul opened the first of the two newspapers he'd brought with him, and flipped the pages to the want ads. Sipping his coffee, he scanned the columns of four different pages and found ads for copywriters, book editors, and newsletter writers, but nothing in the field of journalism that seemed close to a real reporter's job. He put aside that paper and opened the second, hoping for better luck. It was *The New York Daily Tribune*, and he winced at the irony of looking for a new job in the publication of his old employer.

Mary came over to his table with silverware wrapped in a paper napkin and a plate with his toast. She was wearing blue jeans and a white T-shirt that had *Gardening Cultivates The Soul* printed over an impressionistic drawing of colorful flowers. Paul lifted the newspaper and she put them on the table. She put her right hand on her hip, canted it slightly, and said, "Reading the want ads?" as if it were a joke.

Paul felt his ears grow hot and knew they were flushing. "Yeah. Got laid off yesterday."

"You're kidding!" Her tone changed to one of concern. "You're a reporter. They don't lay off reporters."

"They can lay off anybody."

She smiled and lifted her chin in a mock gesture of pride. "Not the waitresses. The lower you are on the food chain, the more essential you become."

He laughed. "You learn that in psychology class? Or are you a business major, too?"

"I learned that in the school of hard knocks," she said with a mock upper-class sniff as she walked away.

She went back to the kitchen and brought out his omelet, putting it on the table in front of him along with the Tabasco. He moved the newspapers to the side so he could read while he ate.

"Bon appetit," she said, using the French pronunciation. Before he could reply she was off in the direction of two elderly women who'd just walked into the restaurant.

Paul opened the Tabasco and poured it over his omelet, took a bite and savored the vinegary hot taste mingled with the feta, onions, and tomatoes of the omelet. With his free left hand, he turned the paper to the comics' section, and then looked down at the far left corner to see what was happening with Doonesbury. It was the continuation of a story theme he'd been reading for the past week, and as he read the panels he didn't notice the man walking by until he sat down in the chair opposite Paul.

"How ya doin'?" the man said, his voice sounding like there was coarse sand in his throat. Paul guessed he was in his fifties, and probably homeless. He had the broad, lined face of Irish ancestry and years of alcohol, broken veins spidering across his nose and cheeks, his fingers cracked and dirty like antique leather that's been left out in the rain for years, his fingernails yellowed and striated. He wore two hooded pullover sweatshirts, the inner one red and the outermost gray, a black stocking cap that barely held in wild strands of greasy gray hair, and as he had sat down, Paul noticed his pants were army camouflage fatigues. The smells of body odor, urine, and wood smoke surrounded him like an invisible mist.

"I'm fine," Paul said, wondering what was going on. After Noah, he was ready for anything.

"Good eggs?" the man said. "I see you like the hot sauce."

"Yeah, they are," Paul said. "You want some?"

"Nah," the man said. "I had my breakfast a few hours ago. Cooked up some grits with cheese, and put a couple of poached eggs on 'em. They're good with hot sauce, too, but you want to get something with a little more character than just that Tabasco. I'm partial to Jo B's Chilipaya, although Odin's Feast makes a great hot garlic sauce, too."

Paul nodded, trying to take in the idea of a homeless gourmet. "Coffee?"

"That's a good idea," the man said, reaching into his pants pocked and rummaging around. He brought out four one-dollar bills, carefully unfolded them, and put one on the table. "I pay my own way. Can collecting was good last night."

Paul nodded and waved at Mary, pointing at his coffee cup and then the man sitting opposite him, and she nodded and headed for the coffeepot.

"My name's Jim," the man said, reaching out his hand.

Paul shook it, surprised at how cold and firm it was, and said, "Paul."

Mary put the coffee cup, a napkin, and a spoon in front of Jim with an undisguised look of disapproval. "Is everything okay?" she said to Paul, not giving Jim any eye contact.

"Anything else for you, Jim?" Paul ignored her implied question. He knew a part of her job that she disliked—but her continued employment depended on—was preventing homeless people from reaching the restrooms. By staking Jim to himself, Paul gave him a bit of respectability, saving her the unpleasant task of throwing him out.

Jim shook his head. "Coffee's fine, ma'am," he said, even though Mary kept her head and eyes pointed at Paul. She looked at Paul and raised an eyebrow, as if to say, *Do you really want to get into this?* so Paul added, "Mine is, too, Mary."

"I'm glad," she said in a neutral tone, giving Jim no encouragement in case there was a next time, and left.

Jim watched her backside for a moment as she walked off with a rigid step, and said, "I don't believe I'll leave her much of a tip. Whatever happened to human civility? I served my country in Vietnam; I paid my taxes for better than twenty years; and I was born in this country, which is more than half the people in this city can say. You know, the poor get no respect."

"Maybe she's having a bad day," Paul said, not wanting to make the situation worse for Mary.

Jim leaned forward as if imparting a secret. "Fact is, Paul, she's afraid. Her deepest fear is that she'll end up, someday, just like me. And the truth is, she's closer to it than she could ever imagine." He picked up his coffee cup and looked at the white steam misting on its surface. "Everybody is, in fact."

"Are you an angel?" Paul said, figuring he may as well just get right to the issue. If it turned out to be a foolish question, at least it wasn't like he'd asked it during a job interview or of a neighbor.

Jim pulled two sugar packets out of the cup on the table, tore them both open, and drained them into his cup. As he stirred the coffee, he looked up at Paul and said, "No, I'm just a human being, just like you."

"How come you sat down here?"

Jim tapped the spoon on the edge of the thick white porcelain mug and carefully placed it on the napkin. He picked up the cup and blew across its top. "You looked like you could use some company."

"Seriously?" Paul took a bite of his eggs. The feta cheese and onions overpowered the smell from Jim's clothes.

"Actually, Joshua said I'd find you here." He pronounced the name oddly, as if it were Yeshua.

Paul swallowed the bite. "Joshua?"

"Guy who lives in the house next to me. At least so far. The mayor keeps siccing the cops on us."

"Why'd he tell you to find me?"

"Said he's got something to tell you."

"Something?"

Jim put his coffee cup on the table in front of him and spread out his hands. "Said you were gonna help us save the world."

Paul was startled to hear Noah's words in Jim's mouth. "How'd you know who I was?"

"Joshua said to look for a young white boy. Said you'd be eating an omelet with lots of hot sauce in the Fashion Coffee Shop, right around the corner from the Fashion Institute. And here you are."

"He know my name?"

Jim shrugged. "I dunno. If he did, he didn't tell me. Just said, 'You find that white boy and bring him to me.' So here I am."

"You're supposed to take me to him?"

Jim grinned and his face wrinkled like a puppet's. "Yep. You interested in coming?"

"Are you part of the Wisdom School?"

Jim smiled. "Life is a school in wisdom, isn't it?"

"Is Joshua an angel?"

Jim looked at his coffee, took a slow sip, put down the mug gently, as if it were fragile. "You'll have to ask him that. You ask the people around him, you'll get all kinds of answers."

"Finish my eggs first?"

"By all means. Coffee refills are free here, so I expect to get at least one for my money."

## Chapter Seven

# Into The Tunnels

Paul and Jim walked west along 27$^{th}$ Street, crossing first Ninth and then Tenth Avenues. The sky was a bright blue between the buildings, the air sharp and cold, a light breeze blowing the smells of car exhaust and the Hudson River into their faces from the west. Buildings behind them and to their left obscured the sun, casting long shadows across the streets. They walked on the right side of the street, occasionally stepping into the sun and feeling its warmth. Paul wore a brown leather flight jacket over a blue work shirt and white cotton sweater, stonewashed blue jeans, and old sneakers. The air was cold, well below freezing, and his ears ached. He kept his hands in the pockets of his jacket to protect them from the cold. The streets were filled with cars, delivery trucks, and taxis, but the only people he saw out walking marched with a grim determination toward the business districts of the city.

Along the way, Jim alternated between purposeful silent marching and chatting. When he talked, he slowed down to a walk, as if marching and talking at the same time were incompatible.

"Where're we going?" Paul said.

"Tunnels."

"You mean the sewers?"

"Nah," Jim said. "Back around the Civil War time, the whole west edge of Manhattan was railroad, running along the Hudson. Tied together the slaughterhouses downtown, the garbage dumps midtown, the warehouses all over from downtown to uptown. Most everything come into the city come in on the rail; weren't trucks back then, and only a couple of bridges. People built shacks all along the tracks, they'd use coal fell off the trains for heat, worked for the railroad or in the dumps or whatever they could find."

They crossed Eleventh Avenue, and Jim waved around at the streets and buildings. "During the Civil War," he continued, "and then again in the thirties when the economy went to hell, this area was miles and miles of shantytown, all up and down the Hudson, with rail tracks running right through it." He waved uptown. "'Bout the mid-thirties, old Bob Moses got the idea to cover over the mud flats uptown, so's the rich folks wouldn't have to look out their windows onto railroad tracks and tarpaper shacks. So they built the promenade, all the way out to the water, and covered over the railroad. It was still there, they just put steel beams and concrete over it, and then built streets and buildings and all sorts of stuff over that. Over the years, it came all the way down here to this part of town, covering over the tracks."

"We're not talking about the subway?"

"No, this is something different. This was the railroad. I think Amtrak owns most of it now, as it's their cops who're all the time rousting people out. Them and the city's finest, dancing to the mayor's tune." The sarcasm in his voice was unmistakable.

"So what happened to the people?"

"Well, most of 'em, back in the thirties, they got run off. Went elsewhere. The railroad had these huge underground tunnels, and uptown they even built concrete bunkers—rooms—into them so the guys who worked on the railroad could live in 'em. The poor guys, you know, who shoveled coal and all. And then the railroads went out of business when everybody started using trucks. This's just in the past fifty years, really. But that's been two generations, and people forgot about the tunnels; the railroad companies that built them are long gone, so nobody knows about them." They stopped at the mouth of an alley between two massive brick buildings, just short of Twelfth Avenue and the river beyond it. "Except us, of course," Jim added with a wide grin.

"You live in the railroad tunnels?"

Jim stood up straight, pulled his shoulders back a bit. "Come full circle, I guess you could say. Back into the womb, if you want to get philosophical, but for me it's back to my teenage years. I was a tunnel rat in Vietnam. Chased Charlie around, underground, climb through these little tiny places, never know when you're gonna find the enemy, a booby trap, or snakes and rats. I didn't much like that, but at least I survived it, although several of my buddies didn't. Anyhow, now I'm back, living in the tunnels again, only this time the war is here in Manhattan, not in Vietnam."

"The war?"

"The war against the poor and the homeless."

Paul nodded, remembering the time just a month earlier when he'd seen a homeless man with a mangy dog sitting on a dirty blanket on Fifth Avenue, up near 60th Street. The guy had a sign made out of the side of a large cardboard box, explaining in red crayon that he was "a permanently disabled Vietnam veteran with Agent Orange poisoning," asking people to put spare change into the green plastic cereal bowl that rested in front of his dog on the blanket. A New York City cop had been walking just ahead of Paul, and as the cop passed the homeless man, he grabbed the sign and tore it in half, then tore it again. Paul stopped walking and watched in horror as the man grabbed his dog and began to cry. The cop marched to a trash basket and stuffed the sign into it, then came over and kicked the man's bowl, scattering the change it in out into the street. As Paul walked off, feeling miserable and powerless, the cop was kicking the man's garbage bag of clothes and personal effects, yelling at him to get up and move on. New Yorkers walking by either pretended not to look or nodded in silent approval of the cop.

"So, here we are," Jim said, walking into the narrow, trash-strewn alley between two large old brick buildings, one now a warehouse and the other a vacant factory. Paul followed him, wondering what was going on; there was no exit from the alley, just a large Dumpster at its end. Was it a trap or a setup? He glanced at Jim's kind face and told himself it wasn't, that everything would be okay.

Jim marched over to the brick wall that was the back side of the empty factory and kicked aside a scattering of loose newspapers, revealing a rusted grating over what looked like a square manhole. He pulled off the grating and set it beside the hole, then gestured at the black opening into the ground. "Our front door," he said with a smile. "Climb down, and I'll follow you and pull the grating back over us."

"Is it safe?" Paul said, feeling a claustrophobic dread as he looked at the silent black hole.

Jim bent over and put his head into the hole, looked around, stood back up, and said, "Nobody down there right now. I'll be with you. Nobody's gonna hurt you."

"And Joshua's down there?"

"Yep. Let's go."

"Are there rats down there?"

Jim laughed. "The size of raccoons. But they won't bother you. It's the humans you gotta worry about, and so long as you're with me or Joshua, you're fine."

Paul walked over to the hole and could see there were rusted inch-thick steel rungs anchored into a concrete wall, each coming out about four inches, descending into the earth and vanishing in the blackness, which was deep and hollow in contrast to the bright day. He climbed down into the hole, his fingers and palms shocked by the freezing steel. His body began to shiver and tremble; when his head dropped below the surface he paused. He could tell from the sounds around him that he was descending into a cavernous area, and, hanging here, he was at least forty feet above the ground below. He took a breath and continued down until his feet hit gravel, then walked back from the rungs and looked around, his eyes adjusting to the dim light, as Jim, above him, pulled the grate back into place and began his descent.

The tunnel was huge, the forty-foot-high ceiling made of row after row of massive steel I-beams, studded rhythmically with round-headed bolts and welds, their texture revealing rust and ancient black paint. The two walls were over a hundred feet apart, and a single pair of railroad tracks followed their ties off into an echoing infinity of distance in both directions. About every hundred yards or so in what Paul believed was the northerly, or uptown, direction, there were gratings over the tracks that allowed sprinkles of sunlight to beam down into the empty tunnel showing an occasional fragment of graffiti on the otherwise clean concrete walls. Southbound was a distant echoing blackness; the track, railroad ties, gravel floor, and cement walls swallowed whole. The air smelled of dust and wood smoke and old coal. The sounds of Jim taking his last few steps and then jumping to the gravel echoed off into the distance, both north and south.

"It seems empty," Paul said. The echoes of his own voice startled him, and he looked around warily at the dim, black-and-white world. Every stone and beam stood out in sharp relief, yet in the dim light it seemed that the world had been drained of its color. The temperature was at least ten degrees warmer than the street.

"This is just the door," said Jim. "We gotta walk about a mile, now." He stepped between the two tracks and began walking south, toward the darkness. Paul looked up at the grate above him, fought down the urge to bolt and climb back up and out, and followed Jim.

They walked into the darkness until Paul was stepping carefully to avoid stumbling. There was still enough light for him to dimly make out the tracks and the walls; the echoing sounds of each step told him where the walls were, but he could no longer make out the stones and railroad ties between the tracks. Jim was absolutely silent, and Paul took that as a cue to keep his thoughts and questions to himself.

His first clue that they were close to habitation was the smell of food. Spaghetti sauce was Paul's guess, with lots of onions, garlic, and oregano. And coffee, some kind of very dark roast, almost an espresso. Then he could hear the faint murmur of conversation. Ahead of him, Jim stopped walking and said, softly, "Take my hand, kid. This is kind of tricky."

Paul could just make out the shape of Jim's body and felt the hand touch his chest before he saw it. He took Jim's hand in his, and Jim led them off the tracks toward the wall to their left. Paul felt as if he were walking on the edge of the world, into a distant blackness, that at any moment he might step off the edge and fall forever. He held tightly to Jim's hand. They came to the wall and walked along with it, Paul reaching out to touch its cold and pebbled surface with his free hand, it keeping him oriented and balanced. After twenty feet or so, Jim ducked down, and Paul realized he was crawling through a hole in the wall, a jagged and irregular opening that somebody had made with a pickaxe. The smell of food was now very strong, and Paul could make out the sound of cats meowing over the soft murmur of human voices.

"This way," Jim said, stepping into the hole. "Just duck and follow me. Watch your head."

Paul followed him through a wall that was ten to twelve feet thick. When they came out the other side, they were in a different set of tunnels, narrower and with closer ceilings. Steel beams arched gracefully up and over from each side, meeting in the center of each of three different track lines like in an ancient, gothic cathedral. Paul guessed he'd just gone from a tunnel built in the early 1900s to a network of ones built sometime before the Civil War.

There was light here, but it showed in cracks and clots of yellow—kerosene lanterns and small wood-fires—and fainter glimmers from small grates above. The air was thick with the smell of smoke, garlic, cooking onions, urine, and tobacco. To their left, three sets of tracks emerged from under a rockslide where the walls had collapsed or been dynamited in some distant era. To their right, each of the three tracks vanished into its own narrow tunnel, each framed by the gothic-arched steel frames.

A series of wooden boxes, every one the size of a Jeep, stood alongside the tracks in each of the three tunnels. The boxes were spaced about ten feet from each other, and in front of one of them four men and a woman stood around a wood campfire over which a grate on cinder blocks held three pans. Strips of what looked like acorn squash on the grate sizzled and dropped sputtering bits of moisture into the fire below, and the pans steamed. There was a card-table next to the fire covered with plates and cups. A dozen chairs surrounded the fire, ranging from old metal kitchen chairs to institutional folding chairs to plush but tattered recliners. This was apparently the community gathering place, Paul realized.

Jim rolled his head toward Paul in a "come with me" gesture and walked to the fire and the people standing in a group beside it. Paul followed.

The fire brought color back into the tunnel, in the area extending ten feet or so back from the flames. Two of the men were black, one young and one old, one looked Hispanic, one looked Middle-Eastern, as if he were Egyptian or Palestinian. The woman was black, perhaps Paul's age, a bit overweight in jeans and several sweaters.

The younger black man wore baggy jeans and several pullover sweatshirts, a watch cap, and expensive basketball shoes. He had a wide nose and round face, large eyes, skin the color of coffee, and long hair in dreadlocks. Jim introduced him as Pete, and Pete said to Paul, "How y'doin, man?"

"Okay," said Paul, unsure what the protocols here were. The five people seemed to have been expecting him.

The older black man had lighter skin, the color of finished oak, and short hair that was shot-through with gray. Jim waved toward him and said, "This is Matt." Matt nodded in Paul's direction, and Paul nodded back.

Jim gestured at the woman and said, "Salome," and the woman smiled and reached out her hand. Paul shook it and said, "Pleased to meet you," and she smiled again, but said nothing in reply. Her handshake was warm and firm, then she stepped back and looked into the fire.

Jim waved at the Hispanic man, said, "This is Juan." The man looked like he was in his early fifties, with a neatly trimmed moustache. His light brown eyes sparkled in the firelight, accenting the smile wrinkles that stretched from his eyes back into his hair and short sideburns. His hair was neatly trimmed and mostly gray. Paul shook Juan's hand and both nodded to each other.

"And this," Jim said, as if he'd been building up to a grand finale, "is Joshua." Again he pronounced it that odd way as he gestured toward Joshua and bowed slightly from his waist.

Joshua looked like the young Middle-Eastern men Paul had seen so often on the news, Israeli soldiers or Palestinian protestors. He stood the same height as Paul, six feet tall, and had olive skin, straight black hair that was cut short on top but ran into a ponytail from the back, a symmetrical long face with striking wide-spaced eyes. He wore old blue jeans with a tear in the right knee, a green cable-knit sweater pulled over a blue plaid flannel shirt, and black army boots. Although poorly dressed, he looked impeccably clean.

"I'm very pleased that you came," Joshua said, reaching out to shake Paul's hand.

"I'm pleased to be here," Paul said, noticing in his peripheral vision that the others seemed to hunch forward slightly and watch carefully as the two shook hands, as if they were expecting something important to happen. He decided to take a wild shot. "Do you know Noah?"

Joshua smiled and stepped back, sitting down in a white plastic lawn chair. "Yes," he said simply. The group around them breathed a collective sigh of relief, as if in Joshua's positive statement Paul had just passed some important test. He added, "Sit down and relax."

Jim pointed Paul to a light-brown cloth-covered recliner with its footrest permanently fixed in the air, next to Joshua's lawn chair. Each of the others took one of the other chairs, forming a small circle around the fire, except Juan, who leaned over the fire and stirred a pot filled with a thick vegetable goulash. Paul sat down, noticing the fabric was warm from the fire.

"You like somethin' to eat?" Juan asked Paul in Spanish-accented English, nodding at the pot as he stood up and stepped back to a chrome-and-plastic kitchen chair, where he sat down.

"I just had breakfast, thanks," Paul said, noticing the unmistakable smell of curry from the largest pot, a tang of onions, garlic, and ginger from a smaller one that seemed to be a sauté of vegetables and rice.

Juan smiled. "This's really lunch, I suppose." He leaned forward and moved the squash strips to the edge of the grill, away from the flames. "Be ready in an hour or two, 'though I could pull you off some now."

"I appreciate the offer," Paul said. "It smells good." The fire warmed his face and hands, and he felt inexplicably relaxed here in this totally alien world he'd ever even suspected existed under the streets of his city.

There was a long moment of silence, everybody looking into the fire. Paul realized it wasn't the uncomfortable type of silence, like Mack would sometimes impose on an editorial meeting to build tension while each person in the room worried they were going to be the object of his next rant. This was, instead, a comfortable silence, the silence of close and trusted friends who enjoyed each other's company. He felt like he was among family, among tribe, with friends who would live and die for each other.

"Joshua," Matt said, drawing the attention of everybody around the circle, "Tell us 'gin 'bout where to look."

Joshua stared at the fire for a moment, then looked at Paul with a totality of attention that made Paul feel as if he was the most important person in the world. "You know about people who come to tell you what to do to find the Kingdom of God?"

Paul nodded. "I think I met one yesterday, on the street. He grabbed my arm and yelled at me about heaven."

Joshua nodded. "If anybody comes to you and says he'll lead you to the Kingdom and says, 'Look, it is in the sky,' then the birds have already preceded you there. And if he says, 'It is in the sea,' then know that the fish were there ahead of you. The Kingdom is inside of you, as well as outside of you. When you know yourself, then others will know you, and then you'll realize that all are daughters and sons of the living God. But if you don't know yourself, or know where the Kingdom is within you, then you live in a place of ultimate poverty, and you, yourself, are that poverty."

"Is that one of the Wisdom School teachings?" Paul said. "I'm not sure I understand it."

Joshua said, "Actually, it's a quote from Jesus, from the Gospel of Thomas." He glanced at Pete, as if to ask him to answer Paul's question.

Pete leaned forward in his chair, a brown metal folding job that looked like it had once seen service in a high school gymnasium. He said to Paul, "There was this guy looking through the dumpsters for food, and he found a little bit here and a little bit there, some lettuce and some carrots and a half a bottle of catsup. And then in the last dumpster he found where the store had just thrown out an entire case of frozen dinners, each one a complete meal, just because something had broken and spilled on the boxes and gotten them dirty. And so the store, they threw that out, these thirty-six complete meals. And when this guy found that case of frozen dinners in the dumpster, he pulled it out and threw into that dumpster all the other stuff he'd collected, and he took that case of food down to his friends, and everybody had all he could eat for two days."

"I'm not sure I understand that, either," Paul said.

Salome lifted a hand off the recliner she sat in and said, "It's a parable, man. The pearl of great price." She held her hand out flat, thumb up, and waved it side-to-side.

"Ah," Paul said. "I get it. Just like Jesus taught."

"Right," she said. "When you get the Truth, the pearl, the case of frozen dinners, then you don't need all that little stuff. You can leave behind your old life."

This wasn't at all like his meeting with Noah, and Paul was thinking that Joshua seemed more like a street philosopher—maybe even a psycho—than an angel or a ghost or whatever.

Paul wondered if Jim had just made up the story about where he'd find the guy with the omelet, and Paul had stupidly gone along with being dragged into some weird little cult of homeless people. He looked around the circle and everybody seemed harmless enough, even friendly, but then people probably thought that about Jim Jones and Charlie Manson in the early days, too.

It occurred to him that maybe he should get out while he still could.

He looked around into the darkness, the maze of tunnels, and wondered if he could find his way out without help. It didn't seem likely. He imagined himself stumbling around in the dark trying to find the tiny hole between the two tunnel systems, running into rats or falling into piles of garbage or sewage. He could feel his heart race.

Salome interrupted his thoughts. "Jesus taught lots of things folks choose to ignore nowadays," she said. "Like He said that if you're gonna save the world, you're going to have to give up the kingdoms of Caesar and join us in a vow of poverty. That doesn't mean you can't have material things or even wealth; it means you're not attached to them. If you lost them, or gave them away, it wouldn't matter. And if you're rich, it doesn't matter. No matter how you live, you carry with you the knowledge that, ultimately, you're always living without ever knowing where tomorrow's food or shelter is coming from, but knowing that God will provide. In the Sermon on the Mount, He said, 'Therefore take no thought, saying, "What shall we eat?" or, "What shall we drink?" or, "Wherewithal shall we be clothed?"' You see? Live in the here and now, just totally present, regardless of wealth or poverty as defined by our culture. Then, and only then, are you living in the hand of God."

Her voice carried a certainty that verified Paul's fear. They thought Joshua was some sort of saint or savior. The guy knew nothing about Noah but had just said he did because Paul had asked with an expectant tone of voice. And Jim had probably brought him down here to recruit him, maybe even to hit him up for money, or maybe something worse.

He turned to Joshua, who was still smiling at him in a way that seemed friendly, but Paul realized could also be psychotic or even sinister. He said, "Why'd you ask Jim to bring me down here?"

Joshua said, "I have cast onto the world a fire, and you can see, I am keeping watch over it, guarding it until it blazes."

"You're a fire?"

"My teachings are a fire."

Definitely Jim Jones stuff, Paul thought. "And you are?"

Joshua pulled his legs up and crossed them, sitting cross-legged on the chair, his spine straight. "There is a light which is above them all, and that is Me. I am the

All. The All came forth from Me, and the All will return to Me. If you split a piece of wood, I am there. You will find Me if you lift a stone."

"Are you an angel?" Paul said.

"You can read the sky and tell if it will rain," Joshua said, his voice growing so soft that Paul leaned forward to hear his words, "but you don't recognize me as I sit before you, and you don't know how to read this moment."

"I'm sorry, but I don't recognize you," Paul said, thinking that he should get out of the tunnel before things got too weird. "I don't think we've met before. Maybe you've mistaken me for somebody else." He glanced over at Jim, but Jim's expression gave away nothing.

Joshua waved his hand at the people sitting around the small fire. "Unto these, my friends, it is given to know the mystery of the Kingdom of God: but unto them that are without, all these things are done in parables, so that seeing they may see but not perceive, and hearing they may hear but not understand."

"Your teachings are secret?" Paul said. Off in the distance over Joshua's shoulder, up the left-most of the three tunnels, Paul saw a light waving in the darkness as if somebody was walking toward them carrying a candle. Juan, sitting just to his left, moved his head as if he noticed it, too.

"Yes and no," Joshua said. "Is a candle brought to be put under a bushel or under a bed? Shouldn't it be set on a candlestick? All the secrets are clear to the person who can hear them, but to those who can't hear, they're only stories. Just interesting, quaint stories."

"Parables."

"Yes, Paul. These are the ways these teachings have been given in the past. Each of my last five answers are words you can also find in the sayings of Jesus, in the Gospel of Thomas. Let me boil it all down for you. There are some who say that you can understand the mysteries of life through knowledge. They seek knowledge, and try to know God through their minds. But all they ever find is their own mind, talking back at them, because the soul of God is not knowable through the mind."

"Noah said something like that to me."

"Yes, he would. That first path, the path of knowledge, is useful and interesting, but to truly know God you must move to the higher path, the path of the mystic. The mystic doesn't seek to know *about* God, but to both touch God directly and then to become one with God."

"And that is done through love?"

"Love and faith," Joshua said. "When your heart's desire is to become one with God, then everything else falls into place. When you're following the correct path, you'll feel a deep peace in your heart. When you're straying from the path, you'll feel turbulence and confusion in your heart. This is the meaning of the parables of the *Pearl of Great Price* and of the *TV Dinners in the Dumpster*. Do you understand, Paul?"

"I can't say I do with my mind, but it feels right to my heart."

"There are three steps to this path, Paul. You'll find them in so many parables, when you realize that this is what they're talking about. The first step is loneliness. Your separateness from God brings you a deep loneliness, which most people misunderstand and our culture tries to translate into a desire for things that can be bought and sold. The second step is love, discovering the feeling of your heart, in one way or another. And the third step is to use the loneliness and love to step into the soul of God. This is when the father throws the feast for the son who left and has returned. Do you understand?"

Paul felt a warmth in his chest that he couldn't explain, like he was falling in love. But with a homeless man from the Middle East? He knew it wasn't that; there was something deeper going on. Yet his mind was rattling on, trying to decipher the logic, trying to understand. And couldn't. "I'm not sure," Paul said.

Joshua stood up and walked over to Paul, squatted in front of him, and drew a circle in the dirt. "This is the barrier between you and God. You are inside the circle,

God is everything outside the circle. Your ego, your incessant thinking, your mind, are what the barrier is made of. That's what the saying that somebody must leave behind their mother, father, brothers, and sisters meant. It didn't mean to literally hate them or leave them, but to realize that all of these ideas that other people are 'other' or 'outside the circle' is wrong. Everything is 'you.' And the 'you' is both you and is God. Paul, *there is no circle, no separateness.*" He stood up and walked back to his chair, sat down.

Paul was speechless. On one level it made perfect sense. On another, it was a prescription for giving away everything and joining a cult or some such thing. He took out his notepad and wrote, *There is no circle, no separateness, between people, each other, and even the entire creation.*

"Paul," Joshua said, "you realize that one day you will die. Right?"

"Yes," Paul said, feeling confused.

"I can tell you with absolute certainty that unless you pass through that circle before then, that moment will be the loneliest moment of your entire life. You will be facing eternity totally alone. But moments after your body ceases to function, you will know a union and love beyond anything you could imagine if you had never passed that circle while you are alive. This is the threefold step—loneliness, love, union. You will do it when you die, but you can also do it now or any time. And then you will never again be lonely. This is one meaning of being 'born again.' It means that you pass through death—the death of that circle, of the barriers of the ego—and enter into a new life. A life of union with God. A relationship of love. And then, in that, you see God's eyes in the eyes of every other living thing; you hear God's voice in the voice of every person, animal, and even the wind; you feel God's love in every moment of life. Do you read books?"

"Yes," Paul said, feeling like he was emotionally gasping for breath.

"People read to know that they are not alone, that others have had the same doubts and thoughts and fears as they. That others are alive, too. It's that first step, again."

"Loneliness."

"Yes, Paul. And then comes love. You realize that all the love you feel is really the love of God, shining through the cracks opened by contact with others. Just like all light on this Earth started as the light of the sun, even the fire there," he pointed to the wood fire that Juan was tending, "which first fell as sunlight on the ground to grow the trees. All light is from the sun. All love is from God. There is no love which is not God's love."

"But what about God's wrath?" Paul said, remembering his years attending church.

"What father, if his son asked him for a fish, would give him a stone?" Joshua said, and Paul recognized the quote from Jesus. "God's wrath is a concept that comes from the Gnostic beliefs, from the anthropomorphic gods men create. The Mystic knows that God's grace—another way to say God's love—is infinite. Only those who think that grace is finite and limited tremble before the choices of life. But when you realize that grace is infinite and absolutely unending, and you learn to listen to your heart for the peace that comes with knowing and loving your Creator and the creation, then the road of life is infinitely full and without fear."

"But so many people say we should fear God."

Joshua smiled. "They are the ones who have not touched the soul of The Creator of the Universe. As Paul wrote to Timothy, 'God has not given us a spirit of fear, but of power and love.'"

"But if God made everything, then there are evil spirits as well as good, aren't there? Isn't it like two sides of one coin?"

"That coin thing is a poor metaphor," Joshua said. "A better one is light. Or sound, as in The Word. Evil is not the opposite of good any more than darkness is the opposite of light, or quiet is the opposite of music. Evil is the word we use to describe the *absence* of that love which is how God manifests. It's a lack of something, not a presence of something else. People who behave evilly are not seized by evil, but have lost their connection to good. They are cold because they are lacking warmth, and do not realize that there is an infinite supply of warmth, if only they knew where to look, how to hear, how to open up to feel."

"That's an astounding thought," Paul said. He took out his notebook and wrote, *It's not two sides of a coin; it's light and dark. The Creator of the Universe is love and good—period. Evil is not 'another god' or another side of the Creator—it's the absence of a connection to the Creator, just like darkness isn't the opposite of light or the other side of light, it's the absence of light.*

He looked back up at Joshua, who was smiling, and said, "What, then, is sin?"

"Sin is not an act against God," Joshua said. "It's an act against yourself. The best definition of sin is that it is any behavior or thought which causes you to forget or lose your connection to the love, the ever-present and in-dwelling presence of the Creator of the Universe."

Juan stood up, pointed past Joshua, and said, "Somebody's coming." Everybody turned to look except Joshua, who said, "It's Mark."

"Hey!" a voice came from the tunnel, and Paul could now see a middle-aged white man dressed in at least two pairs of pants, the outer one gray flannel slacks, army boots, and a grease-stained thick winter coat with faux fur lining the hood. He limped out of the tunnel, holding a Mason jar half-filled with wax and a wick, a candle-in-a-jar, in one hand. The other hand was clutched to his side, where, as he approached the light of the fire, Paul could make out a spreading red stain.

Pete and Juan jumped up and ran over to Mark, loudly asking him what had happened. He clutched his side tightly, his thin long face twisted in pain. "I been stabbed, man," he said in a croak. Juan took the candle from his hand, and Pete put his arm around him and helped him to the fire, sitting him on the ground next to the chair where Joshua sat.

"Ain't no good," Pete said, looking up at Joshua. "He bleeding bad."

"What happened, man?" Matt said, rushing over to Mark as Salome arrived. Only Paul and Joshua remained seated.

"Punks," Mark said, his breath ragged. "They jumped me as I was coming back from Can Do, turning in a bunch of cans. Knew I had some cash."

"Robbed you?" Matt said.

Mark nodded. "They got twenty-three bucks." He turned and looked at Joshua. "I'm hurt bad, man. Can you do something?"

"Do you believe I can?" Joshua said.

Mark nodded and said, "Yeah." Everybody was looking at Joshua, as if expecting some extraordinary thing to happen.

"You're sure?" Joshua said.

"I know you can heal me," Mark said.

Joshua nodded and waved his right hand in the direction of Mark, as if he were polishing a window in the air. Mark gasped and squinted his eyes, then looked at Joshua with a bug-eyed expression of shock.

"Wha' happen, man?" Matt said, his voice thick with worry.

Mark sat up in a single smooth motion. He looked down at his jacket, at the stain, and moved his hand and examined the slash in the fabric, the wet blood on his fingers. Then he slowly unzipped the coat and peeled it off. Under was a bloodstained brown UPS shirt with "Mark" embroidered in a circle over the pocket; below the pocket was another slash. Mark shrugged out of the shirt with the help of Matt, revealing a torn and bloodstained thermal underwear top. He hooked his thumbs under the waistband and pulled it up and over his head, and sat, shivering, naked from the waist up in front of the fire. There was a smear of fresh red blood on the right side of his upper abdomen, just below his ribcage, but no sign of any injury.

Paul watched with a growing sense of alarm, the love he'd been feeling in his heart replaced by a growing turbulence in his mind and stomach. They'd gone to a lot of trouble to stage this, and that had to mean it was part of a Big Con. He felt that the stakes must be very high:

perhaps they'd try to take him for everything he owned. He wondered how many people had been approached in how many coffee shops over the past months. Had any of them been killed after this little band had taken all they owned? Were bodies buried in the dirt all around them? He pushed his hands, balled into fists, into the pockets of his jacket.

Mark stood up with an astonished look on his face, and said to the group, "I was stabbed! I mean real bad, I was stabbed!" He pointed to the center of the blood smear. "Right there; kid musta stuck that thing in five, six inches. I could feel that he'd punctured something big inside, I was leaking on the inside and the outside, I could feel my heart beating all around in there, every time it beat it hurt."

Joshua was smiling and nodding. Matt and Pete were nodding, as if it was just exactly what they'd expected. Juan looked frightened, as if he was thinking about running away. And Salome slowly walked back to her chair and sat down, her thoughts unreadable.

"Was Joshua healed you," Matt said. "He stretch out his hand, he heal you, jes like that." He snapped his finger. "I tell you, you don't believe me. I tell you. You believe me now, man."

Paul was amazed at the quality of the acting, but then reminded himself that good acting was at the core of every con. A million cons a day were run in New York

City, from guys playing Three Card Monty, to guys in boardrooms setting up strip-mines on Indian lands out west, to Susan's ad agency making schoolchildren's happiness depend on their parents buying them the newest video games.

Mark leaned over and put his arms around Joshua's knee, which extended over the edge of his chair. "Thank you, Joshua," he said, his voice cracking. "You saved my life. I was dying, I know it."

"I didn't do anything," Joshua said, his voice matter-of-fact. "It was your faith that healed you, not me."

"But you waved your hand at me, you asked me if I believed."

"If you have faith just as small as a mustard seed, nothing shall be impossible for you. My wave simply brought out your faith."

Paul stood up. "This is wonderful," he said, "and I'm really impressed." Everybody turned to look at him. "I think I've got twenty or thirty dollars on me I'd like to contribute to your work here. But I've gotta get back upstairs, 'cuz if I don't find a job in the next few days, I'll be out on the streets." He looked around, suddenly embarrassed at what he'd just said, wondering if they took it as a value judgement, a negative assessment of their lifestyle. And, if they did, would they use it to move the Big Con along? Did he just open the door even wider, make himself even more vulnerable?

"Who's this guy?" Mark said.

"Friend of Jim's," Matt said, sitting next to him, handing him back his clothes as he re-dressed himself.

Joshua nodded and it seemed that Paul's comment had gone unnoticed by everybody. "We don't need your money, Paul," he said. "In fact, we don't *want* your money." He looked at Jim. "Jim, will you escort Mister Abler back up to the surface?"

Paul felt a sudden dread. "How did you know my last name?" His mind raced back through the morning; he was quite sure he'd never told Jim his last name, and certain he hadn't mentioned it down here.

Joshua shrugged. "There are no secrets when you've touched the soul of God."

It had to mean that the con was set up in advance, that Paul wasn't just the first person who didn't shoo Jim away from his table, but that he'd been set up well in advance. It meant they knew more about him than he'd realized, that he was more vulnerable than he'd thought, that they had their sights on him, their plans lain for him, even before Jim had walked into the coffee shop an hour earlier. Maybe they'd been stalking him for days, maybe even weeks, planning whatever they were planning.

He remembered Rich and his certainty that he'd been given a hallucinogenic drug. What if the same had happened to him? It could explain Noah's popping up, and the whole weird experience of going back in time. But who? When?

Then he remembered the evangelist on the street the afternoon before, the man who'd grabbed his arm just before he'd gone sailing across the street to save the little girl.

That had to be it. The guy was in with them; he even dressed like he was homeless. When the man grabbed him, he must have had some sort of pinprick device that could penetrate Paul's jacket, administering the drug.

He put his left hand over his right upper arm, rubbing it slowly to feel for any sensitive spot, the place where his skin had been punctured. Was it there? He couldn't tell.

"Never no secrets," Matt said, echoing Joshua.

## Chapter Eight

# The Power of Belief

Paul looked around at the expectant faces, feeling like a trapped animal.

He scanned his surroundings, and noticed with a shock of realization that the wooden boxes along the tracks were not packing crates, as he'd originally assumed, but individual residences. The one to his left and behind him had a door half-covered by a blanket, and inside he could see a mattress on the floor, a painting on the wall, a table covered with books and an oil lamp.

These people live here, Paul realized. No rent, no taxes, living off what they could scavenge from dumpsters, getting money by collecting cans and turning them in to recycling centers. Running gauntlets of punks and street gangs to get into and out of their underground world, to get their money safely home from the recycling centers.

*They're poor beyond imagination,* Paul thought, *and they want whatever it is I have.*

He did a quick inventory, remembering that his driver's license, MasterCard, and American Express Card were in his shirt pocket, where he transferred them every morning, along with a gold Cross pen, when he got dressed. It was better than carrying a wallet in a city filled with pickpockets. In his right pants pocket was about fifty dollars in cash; there was another hundred or so back in his apartment . . . if they hadn't already gotten it. Maybe bringing him here was just a ruse to get him out of the way while they stripped his apartment?

"You okay, man?" Jim said, pulling Paul back to the conversation and people around the fire.

"I'm fine," Paul said. "I just need to get back home right away." He pulled his hands out of his jacket pockets, pushed himself out of the recliner, and stood up, flexing his cramped fingers. He'd been clenching his hands in tight fists without realizing it.

Jim glanced at Joshua, who made a tiny gesture, a slight lifting and dropping of his shoulders. "I can take him," Jim said.

Joshua said to Paul in a soft, compassionate tone of voice, "What are you worried about?"

"I need to get back to my life," Paul said. "My apartment, my girlfriend, gotta find a job. I was fired yesterday."

Joshua scratched the smooth skin of his chin. "You're a man of principle."

Paul wondered if their casing of him had included his job at the *Tribune*. "I like to think so."

"You believe in journalistic integrity, and in your own integrity. You believe in the importance and power of truth, although you've also recently come to believe in the importance of power itself."

"I suppose so." That was it, they'd even checked out his employment. He stomped his feet as if he were cold, feeling impatient. "I've gotta go."

Jim stood up.

Joshua said, "Like that time at Richter's store."

"What?" Paul said. The name was familiar, but from a far distant time and place.

"When you were ten. And Alvin Christian stole the little toys off the cereal boxes in Richter's General Store. And you told your father, who called Mrs. Richter."

The memory flooded back over Paul; he hadn't even thought about it in at least a decade, much less ever told anybody about it in his life. Alvin had been so sure it was Paul who'd "squealed" on him that it ended their friendship, and Paul had been tight-lipped about the incident ever since.

He leaned forward and put his hands on the back of the recliner, holding it for balance. "What are you talking about?" he said to Joshua, still unwilling to admit he'd turned in his friend, still certain it was the right thing to do. Alvin wasn't hurt by it; if anything, it was a good thing for him, because it stopped him from going down the road of a lifetime of stealing. Alvin got a spanking from his father when Mrs. Richter called him and he'd found the toys under Alvin's bed. His father had taken him down to the store to return them and apologize, but that was it. It wasn't like Paul had sent somebody to jail or anything.

"You don't remember?" Joshua said. "Your old friend, Alvin Christian?"

"Do you know him?" Paul said, the thought occurring to him that maybe all of this was an elaborate plot by Alvin to get even after nineteen years. Maybe Alvin was one of the homeless himself. Maybe he'd hired them. Maybe he'd written a story or article about it—perhaps titled "My Childhood Betrayal" or "My Humiliation"—and published it in *The New Yorker* or some more obscure publication, and Joshua had read it, seen Paul's name, and sent Jim to check him out, and then bring him here. Stranger things have happened.

"I've never met him in my life, Paul," Joshua said. "Or the time when you were fifteen and your friend Vlado Stevic gave you the answers to that math final exam, and instead of looking at them you thanked him for them and then took them home and burned them, unopened. You are a man of principle."

"How did you know about that?" Paul said, gripping the chair even harder. "I never told *anybody*!"

Around the fire, everybody sat and watched intently, but none seemed shocked. "That, Paul, is another thing you must learn."

"How to read minds or do miracles?"

"How miracles are done. To do them is your fate and your choice. Just as it's your fate and your choice whether or not to join us here, to learn my truths and understand the Wisdom teachings, and then to go out into the world to teach them."

Paul said, "You really do know Noah?"

"Before Noah was, I am."

"You know what he and I did?"

"You visited Nippur."

Paul shivered involuntarily. "He told you?"

Joshua ran both hands through his long black hair, flipping it over the back of his shoulders, and sat back down in his chair. "Do you want to know how to perform miracles?"

"Yes," Paul said slowly, concluding there was another answer for Joshua knowing his last name, his story, his childhood. This was all real. He swallowed hard and pulled his notepad and pen from his shirt pocket.

Joshua looked around the circle of people. "Salome?" he said. "Would you care to tell Paul how miracles are done?"

The young woman stared into the fire for a moment, then looked at Paul. He felt the force of her gaze, and it drew him back around to the front of the recliner, where he sat back down in his former seat. He settled into the soft fabric, feeling his muscles relax and his mind clear.

"You understand about matter and energy?" she said.

"They are the same," Paul said. "Matter is slowed-down energy."

She nodded. "Have you ever blown against a leaf or a blade of grass?"

"Yes."

"What happened?"

"It bent or blew away," Paul said.

"Because?"

"Because of the pressure of my breath."

"Your invisible breath."

"Yes."

"Although that, at least, was invisible matter, being propelled by energy, the energy of the force of the muscles in your lungs."

"I understand that."

"What are your thoughts?" Salome said.

Paul was caught off-guard. "What do you mean?"

"I mean the stuff that runs through your mind constantly. All that talking to yourself about the past, the future, and even the judging of the present. Your *thoughts*, the products of your thinking brain. Are they matter or energy?"

"I don't know, for sure. I'd guess they're energy, right?"

"Can they be weighed? Put in a box? Carried around in the hands of others when you are dead?"

"I don't think so."

"Then they are energy. Do you agree?"

"Makes sense to me," Paul said.

"And all of this around us," she waved at the tunnels, the packing-crate homes, the fire, the people seated in the circle, "is matter, which is also made up of energy, just like your thoughts."

"Yes. It all began as energy, then became hydrogen, then matter, then, eventually, this."

"And thought is a form of energy."

"Right."

"And belief?"

"Isn't that thought? I mean, you have to think that you believe."

Salome shook her head. "No. I'd put belief into a category like love. It's qualitatively different than thinking. You can think *about* belief, but to believe is not to think. It is to believe. Do you understand?"

"Like I can't think love, I can just love?"

"Right."

"Ok, I'm with you. Belief and love are both forms of energy that can run through my brain and body, just like thinking, but they're not thinking. They're different from thinking."

"Right. Just like your breath coming out of your mouth is air, and the room is filled with air, but the breath coming out of your mouth can bend over the leaf you hold by its stem. But the air in the room isn't bending the leaf, because it's not being moved by the energy of your lungs and diaphragm. So your brain can carry the energy of thinking, or the energy of love, or the energy of belief, but they're different."

"Right."

She scooted forward to the edge of her lawn-chair and rested her elbows on her knees. "Actually, thinking pretty much resides in your brain, whereas belief and love encompass your entire nervous system. You feel them in your heart, your stomach, and your muscles. All through your body. You know what I mean?"

"Yes," said Paul, thinking about Susan and feeling his stomach twist. "I know exactly what you mean."

"So love, that energy we call love, that is the connection you have to God. If you've absorbed the Wisdom teachings you've already been given, you understand that. Right?"

"Yes, I figured that out last night."

"Ok, here's an eternal truth: 'With faith, all things are possible.' Belief is the energy that allows you to manipulate other forms of energy. Even those forms of energy which have congealed into what we call matter."

"If you had faith you could say to that mountain, 'move over there,' and it would move," Paul said, remembering the teaching of Jesus from church. He wrote down *With faith, all things are possible* in his notepad, and put it back in his shirt pocket.

"Exactly," Salome said. "Faith and belief mean the same thing, in this context. If you have faith, you can move mountains, heal the sick, raise the dead, and the whole shootin' match."

Paul thought back to a discussion in a philosophy class he'd taken in college about something similar from the end of the eighteenth century. "I remember," he said, "a debate about something like this. Wasn't there a British mathematician who wrote that reality was all energy, and Samuel Johnson got quite upset about it?"

Salome held out her hands. "You gone beyond me."

She glanced at Joshua, who said, "It was George Berkeley, and he was an Anglican bishop and mathematician. They named Berkeley, California after him. He was a friend of Halley and Newton. He suggested that all physical matter was just an idea in our minds. He said, '*esse is percipi*,' or, 'to be is to be perceived.' He was close, but he got stuck thinking that the work of the thinking mind was the same as all other forms of consciousness, and that we're the only ones the universe cares about. It was essentially the old, 'If a tree falls in the forest and nobody hears it, does it make a sound?' argument. It assumes the primacy of humans, which is incredibly arrogant, like the Greek notion that if humans vanished, the entire universe would vanish. And so Samuel Johnson challenged Berkeley by kicking a stone hard enough to hurt his own toe, shouting, 'I refute it thus!'"

"So if we vanished, the universe would continue?"

"It was sure here before we came along," Joshua said.

Paul laughed. "Yeah. Got it. So with the power of my mind I can create miracles?"

"Not *the* power of your mind," interjected Salome. "*A* power of your *being*, your *soul*. Miracles are among the many things your soul can do, but just one of them. This isn't about thinking or understanding or knowledge, which are all *other* powers, and are pretty much limited to your mind. It's about belief, or faith, which involve your mind, your heart, your entire being. You can't do miracles with thinking, but you can with believing."

Paul looked at Salome, at her soft brown face, her ragged clothes, and said, "Can you do miracles?"

She shrugged. "I'm here. I consider that a miracle."

"You know what I mean."

"Frankly, I've never tried. At least the way you mean. Been no need. But I have faith that it's within my ability."

"How'd you come to be here?"

She scratched the side of her face, and brushed her hair back. It was thick and curly, what was called an "Afro" back in the 1960's. "I grew up in a middle-class home in Atlanta. Lot of middle-class black folks down there, people go to good schools, make a good living, talk like white folks." A mischievous grin crossed her face. "'Course, I kin talk jive, too."

"You're bilingual," Paul said.

She laughed. "That's truer than you realize. America has become many different nations, maybe always was."

Paul nodded. "So you came here from Atlanta?"

"Yeah, I came to the Big Apple. Right after I graduated from college, got my degree from Morehouse in marketing and communications, minored in philosophy. And thought I'd come up here where the big money was, good jobs with the big ad agencies, you know the drill. But what I found instead was crack cocaine. Within a year I went HIV positive, then lost my place and was living on the streets, tried the shelters but they're a hellhole, and ended up here. That's it in a nutshell."

"You have AIDS?" Paul said, feeling a deep sadness at Salome's story.

"No, just the virus."

"But it'll come?"

"If I believe it will."

"This is sounding an awful lot like Christian Science."

"Christianity, Judaism, Hinduism, Buddhism, and Islam in general, actually," Salome said. "Or haven't you read the Bible?"

"But I can still kick a rock and hurt my toe."

"And I can still move a mountain."

"Or heal yourself of AIDS?"

"That will be an interesting test, won't it," she said. "I guess there's part of me that figures if I can't, then that's life. There's the paradox of doing your best and still accepting whatever you're given, you know? If you live in love with God at all times, it doesn't matter whether you're living or dying, because it's all God. I *will* die, you know. So will you. Nothing is going to stop that. The question is whether you'll wait until you're dying to fall in love with God, to practice God's presence every moment of your life, or whether you'll do it now, right this very minute. I choose to do it now, so the *when* of my death doesn't matter a whole lot to me, frankly. In a way, I'm looking forward to it, to the adventure. And I don't mean that in any morbid or suicidal sort of way. I just know it's coming, and I'm ready."

"You're ready to die?"

She smiled and looked around the circle, then back at Paul. "Paul, can you honestly say that today would be a good day for you to die?"

"What do you mean?"

She pointed to her face. "I may look African, but I'm part Indian, too. Many of my people are. Do you know the story of what Crazy Horse said when Custer attacked the Sioux at Little Big Horn?"

"No," Paul said.

"Crazy Horse was a man of peace. But Custer had split his army, and part of it he sent in to murder the women and children in the Hunkpapa camp, the southernmost of the Sioux villages near Little Big Horn, to try to frighten and demoralize the warriors. And so Crazy Horse said to his men, 'Come on, Lakotas! Today is a good day to die!' And they charged forth, fully knowing that they would probably die, as the Indians almost always did when they confronted the US Army. So when I first learned that story, I asked myself, 'Is today a good day to die?' and I have to say that the answer was, 'No.' I had too much unfinished business. Stuff with family, stuff with friends, stuff with God. You know?"

"Yes," Paul said. "Today is not a good day for me to die."

"But it will happen," Salome said. "Someday. And that day won't be any better, unless you decide to make today a good day to die. And then every day is a day that you're both in and out of this world. That's when you are born again."

"Born again?" Paul said. "I never understood that, but this way it makes sense."

"When you wake up from the dream of our culture and see the world, the creation, all life as it really is, then you are born into spirit and all things become new," Salome said.

"I've gotta write that down," Paul said, and pulled out his notepad, and wrote, *When today is a good day to die because I'm right with all things and everybody and I feel the love of the Creator of the Universe all the time, and I've woken up from the greedy dream of our predatory culture, then I'm born again.* He read what he wrote to Salome and said, "Does that capture what we've been talking about?"

She smiled. "Very eloquently."

Paul looked at her smile—her beautiful smile—and felt a pang at the possibility of her death. "But why would you surrender to AIDS?" he said. "Why not create a miracle?"

She shrugged. "If it's the way it's supposed to be, I'll do it. Or maybe I'll pass into another consciousness. Or maybe Joshua will heal me. It doesn't much matter. Today is a good day to die, and so will be tomorrow."

"No, you should live," Paul said, realizing as he said it that he didn't want Salome to die because he would miss her, not because he feared death may be a bad thing for her. But, still, Joshua could do miracles. "Why don't you ask Joshua to get rid of the HIV?"

"I'm living in the hands of God. In the heart and soul of The Creator of the Universe. So what Joshua does or doesn't do isn't all that important. All the people Jesus and his disciples healed eventually died anyway. I think he did it more for the teaching, you know? Like with Mark here."

"But Joshua can heal? That was real?"

"Yeah. They say he was born knowing how."

Paul turned to Joshua. "Can you tell me the story?"

Juan let out a loud breath, lifted himself off his chair and, on one knee, stirred the curry pot on the grate.

Joshua said, "Wouldn't you rather continue in your training in the Wisdom School?"

"And it's getting close to time for lunch," Juan added.

# Chapter Nine

# The Manmade Demiurge

"I'm also curious about you," Paul said to Joshua. "Are you an angel or a ghost?"

"I told you before that I am not. I was born of woman, just like you."

"But you're doing miracles, like you're some kind of god."

"Is it not written in the book of Psalms, 'I said, "Ye are gods, and all of you are children of the most High"'?"

"I don't know. Is it?"

"Yes," Joshua said. "And you'll hear Jesus say it in the Gospel of John, too."

"So who are the gods? Us?"

"Now you come close to one of the greatest Mysteries," Joshua said. "Some say that there is only one god in all the universe, and we are just wretched, sinful lumps of flesh. Others who say that there is no supernatural god, but that the gods are the human race."

"Who says that?"

"Well, first off, it's a popular notion among some of your recent religions. More importantly, though, it's a basic tenant, albeit unspoken, of your modern culture. Who but a god would have the temerity, or assume for himself the capacity to destroy the planet?"

Paul said, "I think people just think they're given that right by the One God."

"That's what they say. But it's not how they act. Do you really think that anybody who would genetically alter plants, for example, purely for the sake of making a corporation more profitable, does not believe himself to be a god?"

"I guess it depends on how you define the word 'god.'"

"How about, 'Gods are those who can do anything they want without fear of consequences'?"

"Then we have a lot of gods running around loose. But I thought gods caused storms and struck people down dead and helped people kill their enemies."

"Then technology is your god. You can rain fire from the sky on your enemies, alter the course of mighty rivers, tear down mountains."

"Okay, well that's all in the world when we're alive," Paul said, thinking of the street preacher. "But what about a definition that says, 'God is the one who decides where you go and what you do after you die'?"

Joshua shook his head, as if he were sad. "Do you realize what a pathetic statement that is?"

"Sounds like that god has a lot of power to me."

"But it also means, if that's the only place you're going to put your god, that you've completely stripped him from the world of the living. You've pushed him out, or killed him off, or replaced him with gods you call science or technology or humans."

"I'd never thought of it that way." Paul paused for a moment, reviewing his times in church. "But what about the people who pray for things they want? They pray that God will save their child or give them success in business or sports or whatever."

"Do you really think the Creator of the Universe is going to throw a basketball game toward the team that prays the hardest?"

"They sure seem to think that," Paul said. "Before the game, they're all praying up a storm."

" 'And when you pray, don't be like the hypocrites, for they love to pray standing in the churches and in the corners of the streets, that they may be seen by other people. Verily I say unto you, "They have their reward." ' "

"That's from the Sermon on the Mount."

"Yes."

"In other words, public prayer is just a show of piety.

God isn't listening. Whether it's before a basketball game or grace at dinner or a preacher in a church. Don't pray out loud if you're in public. Is that what you mean?"

"Most often. Jesus did pray in public once, with his disciples, just before his crucifixion. But in that prayer, he said, 'and these things I speak in the world, that they might have my joy fulfilled in themselves.' In other words, there are times when it's appropriate to pray in public, but you must know that your prayers then are for the benefit of the people with you, or for you, but they are not the most direct possible connection to your Creator. That is done in private."

"So how should people pray? What should we say?"

"The best prayer is, 'Thy will be done.' Said in secret, because you know God and love God and trust God."

"And who is the God who hears that?"

"That brings us back to the earlier point. The fundamentalists say that humanity is sinful and not at all divine. God is entirely out there and," he pointed to his chest, "not at all in here. Some of the New-Agers, on the other hand, say that God is entirely in here and not out there at all. In other words, we are gods. Those are the two extremes of the argument, and both break down when you examine them carefully."

"So who or what or where is God?"

Joshua stood up. "You must know, you must see, you must hear this truth: any attempt to envision a sentient god will only create an anthropomorphic projection, a man-like god. In other words, The Creator of the Universe is greater than any human can imagine or describe."

"What does 'anthropomorphic' mean?"

Salome leaned forward. "It's like when people think that their dog understands everything they say. They're projecting human qualities into something that's not human. To anthropomorphize a god is to do the same thing."

Paul said, "So when we try to imagine who or what a god is like, we use ourselves as the template, just like when the old lady downstairs has long conversations with the pigeons she's feeding and thinks they understand her?"

"Yes," Joshua said. "When people try to define a god, they usually do it so they can have that god do, say, or take credit for something which will benefit them. And so they create a man-like god."

"And, presumably one who is a member of their particular congregation," Paul said, trying to lighten the conversation. He took his notepad out and jotted down, *The Creator of the Universe is greater than any human can imagine or describe.*

"This is not a joke," Joshua said. "The Creator of the Universe does not say, 'I think I'll kill this child with a cyclone, and save this woman with a miraculous cure of her cancer.' The Creator of the Universe doesn't intentionally condemn these people to starve, and bless these others over here with incredible riches or victory in battle."

"Where, then, did that idea come from?" Paul said.

"Most recently, from the Romans via the Greeks," Joshua said, "although several other city/state cultures came up with similar ideas. The question the Greeks asked themselves three thousand or more years ago was, 'Why is there suffering in the world?' They couldn't explain why they had accidents, disease, defeats in war, earthquakes, floods, crop failures, and the whole thing. At least with natural phenomena like volcanoes erupting, they were pretty sure that people weren't doing it, so they concluded it must be the gods."

"Some cultures think people cause those things?" Paul said.

"Oh, sure," Joshua said. "It's the basis of the idea that people can cast evil eyes or throw curses, that sort of thing. But the Greeks were pretty sure that it was the gods. One story was that a lot of what we saw was a spillover from battles between the gods. They'd get in fights with each other, and the result would be an earthquake. The old 'when elephants fight, the mice get trampled' theory. But most Greeks didn't really believe that. They believed, instead, that there were really two 'creator' gods. One was the Creator of the Universe, who was remote and inaccessible. He produced some supernatural beings, called Aeons, one of whom was a virgin named Sophia. She, in turn, gave birth to a twisted god, which was called the Demiurge. The Demiurge was, essentially, psychotic. Nuts. He was a sadistic crazy. But because he was a god, he had the power to create, so he created this world, just to populate it with us, so he could then torture us. This is how the Greeks and Romans explained the fact that life often includes suffering."

"Whereas the Hindus said people suffer because of bad karma?"

"Yes. There is a law of equality, but when India was conquered by the Indo-Europeans about four thousand years ago, the concepts of karma and reincarnation were refined into the caste system. This allowed the rich to smugly assert that they were rich because they'd lived well in a past life and the poor were wretched because they'd done something wrong in a past life."

"Blame the victim," Paul said.

"Yes, like those today who preach that people get cancer because they're repressing anger, while ignoring the toxic chemicals in our environment. Repressed anger has been around for all of human history, but the explosion of cancer has only corresponded with the industrial revolution, the rise of corporate kings and their rape of the Earth. Similarly, the dominators of ancient times in India, the Hindu kings and priests, justified their domination with the idea of karma."

"So instead of blaming a god for their misery, the poor were told to blame themselves."

"Exactly. Notice that in both cases—the ancient Roman and the ancient Indian—the blame for the wretched lives of the poor is directed away from the dominators, away from the kings and priests and rich people. It's not even an allowed topic of discussion, the truth that people stealing or accumulating wealth while those around them are starving could be a cause of human suffering. The dominators claim they never cause misery. It's always either the individual's fault, or is because of a crazed god."

"The Demiurge."

"Right. That's who it was for the Greeks and Romans, who created the foundations of our culture. Earthquakes, famines, plagues, droughts, disease, birth defects, defeat in battle, and all that sort of thing. It was all the Demiurge, having his fun."

"Sounds like a nasty god."

"And a jealous one, which kept the attention of the people on the Demiurge and away from thinking that maybe the rich and powerful were part of the problem. The Greeks weren't the first to have this idea, as you can guess. Because the Demiurge was so fearsome, other groups with the same idea but a different name for the Demiurge spent much of their time trying to placate him, so he wouldn't torture them even worse. They built monuments and temples to him, made sacrifices to him, killed animals and people, all sorts of things. The more valuable something was, the more they'd want to give it to the Demiurge, in the hopes he'd realize its importance and that would keep him quiet for a few months. So things like their best animals, or their firstborn sons, were included in the sacrifice list."

"And this is one of those 'created in the image of man' gods?"

"Yes. Created in the image of psychotic man, coming out of a psychotic culture, a culture of death and domination. Domination of women by men, of one people by another, of the planet by humans. A culture of slavery. With the Demiurge as the ultimate slave-holder and dominator."

"It's still with us."

"Yes. But every now and then, so the Greeks and Romans thought, the Creator of the Universe, from far, far away, would have his virgin, Sophia, give birth again. And her son, a divine being or incarnated Greek god, would come to the Earth to tell people the secrets that they could use to protect themselves from the wrath of the Demiurge. He was the carrier of the secrets that mere mortals could use to deflect the tortures of the Demiurge. These secrets, or secret knowledge, came to be known by the Greek word for knowledge, which is *gnosis*."

"Is this where the Gnostic religions come from?"

"In large part. The word has been misused for a long time."

"And why such religions have an emphasis on secret knowledge and rituals of initiation, and also why they are all about saving people from an angry god?"

"Yes. If you read the words attributed to Jesus in the Bible, at least the vast majority of them, you'll find that they're not Gnostic. He doesn't speak very much about how to avoid the wrath of the Demiurge, or when he seems to it's almost like somebody tacked something onto the end of another teaching. Instead, most of his teachings are about Mysticism. How to use that highest form of consciousness or energy—love—to connect directly to the Creator of the Universe. But it appears that Gnostic beliefs heavily influenced the apostle Paul. He was born a Roman citizen, not a Jew, and therefore was raised with the Roman ideas of a Demiurge-like god. So it just made sense to him that Jesus had come along as the incarnation of the Gnosis to save people from the Demiurge; you can see it over and over again in his writings. And, of course, this was the world-view of the Romans when they took over Christianity in the third century. And those same Romans then decided what would and wouldn't make it into the text of what we call the Bible."

"But," Paul said, "the world *can* be a terrible place. People do have wars and plagues, and most people live what Thoreau called 'lives of quiet desperation.' If this isn't because the Demiurge is sadistic, or the One God is angry with us, why is it?"

Joshua looked around the circle. "Juan, what do you think?"

Juan stood up and stepped back from the fire where he'd been absentmindedly stirring the pot of curry, and sat in one of the brown metal high-school gym chairs. He looked around the circle, then gestured to the grate most directly above them. "Up there, the world ees crazy, you know? People kill you. They rob you. They steal whatever you have. The kids, they hurt you for fun. I say it's the people who are bad."

Pete shook his dreadlocks and spoke for the first time since he'd met Paul. "If people be so bad, man, howcome you and me be here? We ain't bad."

"We brothers," Matt added.

Mark nodded and made a soft sound of assent through his nose.

Salome's leg bounced up and down a few times and she put her hand on it and said, "You guys don't get it. It ain't the people who're bad, and it ain't the one who made us. It's that culture out there," she waved at the grate. "That's what's bad. That's what sick."

Pete said, "They fixin' to kill off the whole world."

"But," Paul said, "a culture is just made of people. How can it be any different from its people?"

Salome said, "If culture just reflects human nature, then all cultures would be the same. That is not the case. There have been peaceful, nurturing cultures in history. There still are today, although they're being wiped out by us. It's not human nature that is broken or sick, it's our culture, which has spread across most all of the world. The culture of domination and conquest. Of the thousands of tribes on the Earth, only one has gone so insane that they'd lock up food and make people work like slaves to earn it. And that tribe, that culture, is ours."

Paul nodded, noticing how she shifted her accent depending on whom she was addressing. She was bilingual. And probably at least bicultural. "Then what's going on? Why are so many people acting so crazy? And how did Jesus think he could bring peace to such an insane culture as the world the Romans ruled?"

"He started a revolution," Joshua said when Salome glanced at him as if she wanted him to answer that question.

"A revolution?" Paul said.

"Yes, exactly. And it was successful, until it was taken over from within by the very Romans he was revolting against."

"How did he start a revolution?"

Joshua raised his left hand. "Two thousand years ago, before toilet paper was invented, people used their left hands to clean themselves. They'd then dip their fingers into a bowl of water to clean them, but their left hands were never really clean and they knew it. You know that?"

"I never thought about it," Paul said, dizzied by the sudden change in topic.

"It's true," Joshua said, putting his hand back on the arm of his chair. "In fact, it's still that way in most of the Third World. Today, this is how about four billion people live, without toilet paper. And in those lands today, as back then in Israel, the most terrible and vicious way you could insult a person would be to touch him with your left hand. Even gesturing with the left hand was banned in most societies. Among the Jewish Essenes, gesturing with the left hand would earn you a week's banishment from the community. And if you wanted to really insult somebody, to totally humiliate him, particularly in public, you would slap him with your left hand. You understand?"

"Yes," Paul said. "Like giving somebody the finger today."

"More like giving them the finger and spitting in their face," Joshua said. "Or throwing urine on them. Remember where that hand was. You'd only do that to a person you knew couldn't retaliate, right?"

"Unless you wanted your butt kicked."

"Right. So slapping somebody with your left hand, in ancient Roman society, was both the ultimate insult,

and also something that was only done to the most powerless people. The Jews whose land was occupied by the
Romans, for example. There was no recourse for them,
unless it was to punch that person, which would mean
they'd get the death penalty for hitting a Roman citizen.
You understand?"

"Yes," Paul said.

"Unless they could get that Roman to hit them with
his right hand, which meant that a fight was engaged.
Then they'd be justified to fight back. But the Romans
didn't hit slaves with their right hands, they insulted
them by slapping them with their left hands and then
laughed at the humiliated slave who couldn't slap
back."

"Got it."

"So," Joshua said, "which cheek would I strike you
on if I wanted to humiliate you by slapping your face
with my unclean left hand?"

Paul looked at Joshua's left hand, and then visualized
it moving through the air, imagining where Joshua's left
palm would fall. "You'd hit my right cheek if you swung
with your left hand."

"The ultimate vicious and humiliating insult, hitting
your right cheek with my left hand."

"Yes."

"And if you then challenged me to hit you with my
right hand, that would be a challenge to my authority if I

was a slaveholder or a powerful person in your society, right?"

"Absolutely. You'd be saying, 'If you have any courage, you'll start a legal fight with me where I can fight back. You'll hit me with your right hand. I dare you.'"

"And yet it would not be hitting back, it would be merely exposing the evil of the left-handed slap for what it was."

"I understand," Paul said.

Joshua said, "Ye have heard that it hath been said, An eye for an eye, and a tooth for a tooth: But I say unto you, That ye resist not evil with evil: but whosoever shall smite thee on thy right cheek, turn to him the other also."

"Wow," Paul said as he realized what he was hearing. "He *specified* the right cheek."

"It was no mistake," Joshua said. "Here's another. In Roman times, the Roman soldiers and citizens were allowed by law to force a resident of an occupied country to carry something for up to one mile. But the Romans knew well that if they let their citizens and soldiers over-exploit the peoples of occupied lands, it could lead to uprisings and rebellions. So they had very severe penalties if a Roman soldier or citizen forced a slave or person in an occupied country to carry anything more than one mile. A Roman soldier or citizen would lose his citizenship for such an offense, because it could be so destabilizing. And if he lost his citizenship, then he, himself, became a slave."

"Makes sense," Paul said.

"So if a soldier came along and ordered you to carry his belongings for two miles, he was risking his life. If anybody even *thought* that he'd made you carry something for two miles, his life was in danger. You understand? If there were some way you could make it look like he'd forced you to carry something for two miles, you would have put his very life at risk. And if all the slaves or peoples of an occupied country could figure out how to make it look like the soldiers and Roman citizens were violating these anti-exploitation laws, it could cause the local Roman occupying government to topple. At the least, the local Roman governor would risk losing his head. Do you see what I'm talking about? Do you hear what I mean?"

"Yes, of course."

Joshua leaned forward and dropped his voice an octave to say, "And whosoever shall compel thee to go a mile, go with him two."

"It's a call to rebellion," Paul said, astounded.

"Yes. But a passive rebellion, like Gandhi's and Martin Luther King's. Remember, fight not evil with evil."

"This is incredible."

"There's more. In ancient Roman times, the average person owned two pieces of clothing. There was the cloak, which cloaked the body, what today you'd call a robe or tunic or toga. And there was the coat, the warm outer-garment. In Palestine, the days are hot but the nights are cold so people slept in both pieces of clothing, whereas during the day they walked around just wearing their cloak. You with me so far?"

"Didn't most people have several pieces of clothing?"

"Not the people of an occupied country," Joshua said. "The Romans taxed them into poverty. And remember, clothing was made by hand. Every thread was spun by hand, every inch of the garment sewn by hand or on a simple loom. Clothing was incredibly expensive, so most people had only their cloak, for daytime wear, and their coat to wear over that at night and to sleep in."

"Okay, I understand."

"And if you were a slave, or indentured to somebody so you were forced to work for them, during those times there was one most common way the slave-owner would assert his ownership of you. That was to keep your coat during the day while you worked, so you'd have to come back to the slave-owner at night to get it back, so you could stay warm and sleep in it."

"I didn't know that."

"Read the history of the times. It's there. Along with that, there's also the fact that another of the Roman anti-exploitation laws was that you couldn't take a person's cloak, his daytime garment. If you did, he'd be naked. That was both a violation of modesty laws and of public decency, which you'd be responsible for since you took his clothes. It would be an 'over-exploitation' of the worker class, and thus destabilizing to the Empire. You can imagine how people would react if you were to go up on the streets of New York and find some homeless guy sleeping by a building and strip him of all his clothes so he was completely naked. People who never in their lives gave a hoot about the homeless would be outraged. TV reporters would come to the scene to show what a callous brute you are. People would mobilize to help the poor homeless person. Can you imagine?"

"Yes, easily."

"So, say I'm a Roman citizen and I live in a Roman occupied land, and I see you out working in your field and think you'd make a good slave to help me build my new home. All I have to do is go to the local magistrate's office and get a lawful order that you have to work for me. The court order would stipulate that you have to give me your coat for safekeeping every morning as evidence of my ownership of you, and that at night I have to return it to you so you could sleep in it. This happened daily in ancient Roman-occupied lands like Israel was during the times of Jesus. And if you resisted my claim of ownership of you by not giving me your coat, I could have you thrown in prison or fed to the lions."

"Pretty drastic stuff," Paul said.

"So how would you resist?"

"I don't know."

Joshua lowered his voice and said, "And if any man will sue thee at the law, and take away thy coat, let him have thy cloak also."

"That's so ingenious!" Paul said, feeling a sudden burst of revelation. "If I gave you my cloak, I'd be standing naked in front of you. Everybody would think you'd broken the anti-exploitation laws. You'd be at risk of going to prison instead of me."

"Right. And if enough people did it, you'd overthrow the dominators, the Roman government."

"No wonder the Romans killed Him."

"No wonder," Joshua said softly. "And now it's time for us to step forward with the same message."

## Chapter Ten

# All The Lonely Angels

"But how," Paul said, "does this relate to the question of whether our culture is so screwed up, and whether that's because human nature is evil or we're being punished by an angry god?"

"It's at the core of that question," Joshua said. "It points out that it's not the people who are evil. In fact, they're capable of resisting evil without ever having to resort to evil. And it's not a god who's crazy or evil, and the world wasn't created and isn't run by the Demiurge. The insanity is in the *culture* that's taken over. It's the culture that's gone crazy, not the people and not the Creator of the Universe."

"But all the religions say that human nature is sinful, and that we're being punished for that by the One God."

"Not all the religions. Just those religions that serve the people-dominating or slave-keeping cultures. You'll not find those notions anywhere in the vast majority of religions of tribal peoples. You'll not find those notions in the history of the pre-city-building peoples. The biggest problem the missionaries had with the Indians here and the Aboriginal people in Australia was in convincing them that they were sinful and that God was angry at them, and therefore they needed the Church to save them from God. Such ideas only come along when somebody rises up and says, 'I'm taking over and you all have to do what I say. And step one of that is that you all have to work all day to make me richer and more powerful. And if you don't pick that cotton, you'll suffer and it won't be my fault; it's because my god loves me more than you and so made me rich and you poor, or it's because it's your karma, your fault.'"

"A religion of domination."

"Exactly. It's only natural that a culture of domination, of slave-holders, would produce religions of domination. Would sanction caste systems. Would say that people are poor because of something they, themselves, did in a past life and not because the power-holders in the culture have gone insane with greed and power. Would blame some ancient woman for the pain people experience, rather than the kings and wealth-holders."

"But we don't have slaves today. How come this persists?"

"You don't have slaves?" Joshua said. "What is a slave, but a person who owes his life to another. In the city above you are millions of slaves. The corporations who own them even buy and sell them with their properties, just as in the old days. And when they don't need the slaves they acquire with new properties—new businesses they buy—they expel them, leaving them alone and frightened to fend for themselves, just as they did in days of old."

"We're slaves?"

"Do you know anybody who works for a big company or government who would describe himself as 'free'?"

"You mean free cultures don't have religions that blame bad things on god or on the person himself?"

"No, they don't, by and large."

"But what about people who experience supernatural things," Paul said. "Evil things. Ghosts or the devil. Or good things, for that matter, who see angels? I thought that evil was the absence of good or love, so none of those things could be real. But it sounds like what you're saying is that evil is in the culture when it's taken over by a small number of evil people, but that it doesn't exist on a spiritual level."

"Now you're getting close to a greater wisdom," Joshua said. "Although instead of calling them 'evil people,' I prefer to call them 'sleepwalking people.' They're still asleep in the dream of our culture. They don't yet know wisdom.

"Which is?" Paul took his notebook back out. He was thinking that instead of a newspaper story, there was enough here to make a book. They gave Pulitzer Prizes for books, too.

"The Creator is the formless behind the form, encompassing everything, interfering with nothing. However, if enough people believe—or one person believes enough—it is possible to bring from the formless a 'spiritual' form, demonic or angelic, gods or demons, spirits or sprites, angels or ancient beings. All are human creations, as they represent projections of human consciousness, but all are real, nonetheless. The Mystery is that *gods and angels and demons are the creations of humans.*"

"This is getting really confusing," Paul said. "Do you mean to say that if there were no people, there would be no angels, for example?"

"No human-like angels," Joshua said.

"What other kinds are there?"

"What other kinds of conscious beings exist in the billion billion billion worlds of the universe?"

"I get it," Paul said. "Do dogs have dog angels?"

Joshua smiled. "I don't know. I'm not a dog."

"So I created Noah?"

"No," Joshua said. "But someone—possibly he, himself, when he lived as a human—or some group of people provided the belief that allows him to exist. Remember the power of belief."

Paul thought back to his first encounter with Noah, and said, "I think he said something about that."

Joshua shrugged. "He understands how it all works."

"So, then, this means that the Demiurge, an angry god, demons, angels, fairies, the whole range of spiritual beings, that they are real? I mean, even though we made them, they exist? They're *really* real?"

"Yes. It is stated this way. It is possible—paradoxically—to 'prove' there is an intervening spiritual realm and that there are spiritual beings, because with belief or prayer or ritual people *can* bring forth from the formless their own projected forms. And so it is real and true that people like Katherine Kuhlman could perform miracles, that Biblical stories could be true, that Hindu fakirs can be in two places at once, that the Virgin Mary can heal people who pray to her, and so on."

"But I thought that when we attempt to envision a god, we create a man-made or man-like god."

"These two truths do not contradict each other. People built these tunnels. It doesn't make them not-real. You can still die in a tunnel collapse, or hurt your head banging against the iron beams, or find protection and shelter here."

"But there's such variety between cultures when they talk about their supernatural beings. I mean, the Irish have their fairies and the Norwegians their gnomes and the Native Americans have animal spirits . . ."

"Each reflected the culture which created it. And, when you talk with the people of each of those cultures, they will assure you that their creations are real. And they are, just as this tunnel is real. *Gods and angels and demons and all the others are absolutely as real as any other reality.*"

Paul wrote down in his notepad, *We, or our culture, can create supernatural things, but that doesn't mean they're not real, anymore than the buildings and cars we create,* and put it back in his shirt pocket. He looked around the circle and said to Pete, "Do you all understand this?"

Pete said, "I don' need to unnerstand; I just believe, ya know? I live in the love of The Creator of the Universe."

"Yeah," Paul said.

"I mean, I seen Joshua do this stuff," Pete continued. "I don't care how, I jes seen it, and so I believe. I feel it. Dat's 'nuf fo' me." He pointed to Joshua with an exaggerated swinging gesture and added, "I die for dat man, you know? He my man."

"Got it," Paul said.

"I'm with Pete," Matt said. "But I also understand what Joshua says. This ain't rocket science here."

"I think it would be to most people," Paul said. "It seems to me that most people want everything real simple, spoon-fed to them."

"This *is* simple," Salome interjected. "You ever try to make sense of the difference between the Baptists and the Seventh Day Adventists? I tell you, my mother was Baptist and my father Seventh Day Adventist, and there was never a moment's peace between the two of them. Talk about making the simple into something complex."

"You want power over others," Mark said, "you make it complicated. You put yourself between people and the Creator of the Universe or whatever gods you claim exist. You make it so only the priests can figure it all out, and they got to go through years of study to get there. You tell the common people that if they don't do it your way, they're gonna burn in hell. Then you got the church, you know? And *that's* complicated."

Paul looked at Joshua. "What about Jesus, then? Who was he?"

Joshua sat up a bit straighter in his chair. "He is the living son of the Creator of the Universe."

"The Messiah?"

"'Messiah' is a Hebrew word that means 'anointed.' Every king the Jews had was anointed; it was how they were certified as the king. The high priest poured oil on his head, just like in the Twenty-Third Psalm. There were lots of messiahs before Jesus; he claimed the lineage. David was called messiah, as was Saul and Absalom and Solomon and so on. The anointed one was the king, the ruler of the Middle-Eastern tribe that called itself Jews."

"The savior?" Paul said.

"If you believe in the Demiurge, like the Greeks, Romans, and Paul did, then the messiah's job is to save you from the Demiurge. If you want to be saved from the domination of the Caesars, then Jesus gave specific instructions about how to walk away from the kings and the Caesars. Look what he told his disciples about how they should live. That they shouldn't carry money or spend their lives trying to become rich, shouldn't store up food, should pray in private and not in public. Those lessons are still applicable today as if you want to be free of the modern kings and Caesars, although you can search this city's churches from one end to another and you will not find any preacher living as Jesus instructed. Nonetheless, in either case, I'd say the answer is a definite 'yes.'"

"And if I don't believe in the Demiurge and I don't mind being oppressed by the modern-day kings and corporate Caesars?"

"Then you have nothing to worry about, but it's the confidence a dreaming man has when he thinks his dream is real. Remember the parable of the man who built his home on a foundation made of sand."

"So Jesus *was* the Son of God."

"Yes," said Joshua. "As am I and as are you. And so we, now, must awaken people to save the world because the kings are not only oppressing the people, but they are endangering All Life. They are tearing out the heart of our Mother Earth Herself. The stakes are even higher now than they were two thousand years ago."

"Does that mean I'm a messiah?"

Joshua shook his head. "No. You can't imagine how difficult that would be, how much self-sacrifice is involved. The first must be last, must become the least."

"Is this the Greatest Spiritual Secret of the Century?"

"No," Joshua said. "This is common knowledge that any scholars of ecology or Biblical times can tell you. You are not yet ready for the Secret."

"When will I be?"

"That is not for me to know," Joshua said. "I've given you my part."

"Who's hungry?" Juan said as he pulled a box of mismatched plates and silverware from under his chair.

## Chapter Eleven

# Rich's Revenge

When Paul entered the lobby of his apartment building on Eighth Avenue, Billy, the elderly security guard, wasn't in the lobby. It wasn't so unusual, Paul thought, reflecting on other far more unusual oddities, such as he'd experienced in the tunnel. After sharing a vegetable curry and spaghetti with the small group and what had essentially been small-talk, Jim had escorted Paul back to the larger tunnel and the grate so he could head back home and start his job-search.

Paul stopped at the rack of mailboxes near the elevator and opened his. Inside were several pieces of junk mail, a yellow slip from the Post Office informing him he had a registered letter from the building's co-op association that he needed to go sign for, and a letter from the Internal Revenue Service in a white window-envelope.

He pushed the button for the odd-floor elevator, noticing from the indicator that it was coming down. When the doors opened, Billy stepped out. When he saw Paul he looked startled and embarrassed, muttered, "Hi," and walked by with fast, short steps while carefully keeping his attention on the floor.

Odd, Paul thought, as he stepped into the elevator and pushed the button for twenty-one. On the way up, he opened the letter from the IRS and discovered that the pleasure of his company was requested for a full audit of his returns for the past three years. It would be a nuisance, but he didn't have anything to worry about; he hadn't used any odd tax dodges or anything like the rich folks did. He just claimed the standard deduction and sent about a third of his total income, in various forms, to the government. As the elevator went up, he remembered last year's *Taxpayer Freedom Day*. It was proclaimed by some organization he couldn't remember, and some time in May they said that the average taxpayer had been working from the first of the year until that day for the government and now could begin working for themselves. He wondered how much the Roman conquerors had taxed people two thousand years ago. A tenth of their wealth? A third? Half? Three quarters?

The thought brought to mind the conversation he'd had with Jim when they were walking back to the grate.

"You gonna go back to pushing rocks up the side of the pyramid?" Jim had said.

"What do you mean?" Paul had said, as they walked down the long, empty tunnel.

"I mean like the Pharaoh. Moses set his people free. He said, 'We're not gonna take this any more. Build your own damn pyramids.' You know what I mean?"

"I guess."

"Like Bob Dylan said, 'I ain't gonna work on Maggie's farm no more.' He understood. Do it my way or hit the highway. So, you gonna go back to work for the pharaoh?"

"You mean get a job?"

"Yeah. Work for somebody else. Let them run your life. You gonna?"

"Really, Jim, a regular paycheck lets me run my own life. I think if I'm going to join you guys in trying to share Joshua's message, I need that kind of support. I mean, without it, I'd have to depend on the government for welfare."

"I don't get welfare," Jim said, a sharp note of pride in his tone.

"And you live in a packing crate in the tunnel," Paul said, careful to keep his tone matter-of-fact. "I'm sure it's fine for you, but I think I can do more to influence the world from an apartment up above the street. And I've gotta have money to pay for that."

"You saying that apartment is worth trading your soul for?"

"It's not like they're taking my soul," Paul said. "Just eight hours a day, more or less."

"And what else is your soul? What is your life?"

"All the other stuff! My social life, friends, maybe a wife someday, kids, TV in the evening, go to the theatre, read a good book. It's all my life."

"Are you sure?" Jim said. "I work about an hour a day. Two hours on a bad day, when there ain't many cans to be found in the trash. Get the food and money I need in an hour or two. That's about the same workload as most tribal people have, you know? The rest of the time, I spend with my friends, or reading, or thinking. Getting ready to spread the word, when Joshua says the time has come."

"Must be nice," Paul said, reflecting that in the past year or two he'd lost touch with all the people he'd once considered friends. Nobody had the time anymore for anything other than work, it seemed. At least among those who were climbing the ladder.

"So it's back to work for the pharaoh?" Jim said, coming back to the question as if Paul had seriously reconsidered it.

"I guess. Until I'm stable and can publish some of this stuff."

"You could always start your own business."

"I don't know how to do that," Paul said.

"I got mine. 'Jim's Can Service.'" He laughed, then grew serious. "No taxes, no boss, no rules except those imposed by the real world. No bull to take from anyone, and I got friends who'll die for me. Don't got to give any of what I earn to the pharaoh, and don't got to lift stones up the side of the pyramid for him."

"It sounds like a good life," Paul conceded, although he was thinking about what it would be like if he'd ever tried to explain to Susan that he was living in a packing crate in a tunnel under the city. It was unimaginable.

"It's sure better than the army and better than any of the other jobs I've had over the years. I'm not saying it's easy, but it's my life, you know? Nobody else runs it but me."

"I understand, but I don't mind the slavery, I guess."

"Well, brother," Jim said with a wink, "remember what the working girls say. They can buy your body, but that money don't mean they get your heart or soul."

"I'll keep that in mind," Paul had said as the subject ran to its end.

The elevator hit twenty-one and opened, and Paul walked to his apartment door, the mail in one hand and his keys in the other. As he put his key into the dead-bolt lock, he noticed that the metal looked shinier than it had before. Like it was a new lock, or had been scrubbed clean with steel wool. *Odd*, he thought, as he tried to turn the key.

It wouldn't move.

He jiggled the key from side to side, up and down, but nothing helped; it wouldn't open the door. He tried his other key, for the lower lock and doorknob, and found that it didn't work, either.

Paul pulled out the key and walked over to Rich's door, knocking on it in a quick rap-rap-rap imitation of Rich's knock. He heard somebody walk to the door, saw the flicker in the peephole.

"Yeah?" came Rich's voice from behind the door.

"Rich, it's me. Paul."

"So?"

"So my key doesn't work."

"Of course not. You're evicted."

"What?" Paul shouted, his voice echoing down the hall. "What are you talking about?"

"I warned you," Rich said. "But back he came, still asking if I wanted to sell my soul. So I did what I had to do."

"You got me evicted?"

"This joke's gone way too far, buddy."

"Rich, open the door and let me in. Let's talk about this."

"You better go, Paul. Your stuff will be downstairs on the loading dock tomorrow at noon."

"Rich!"

He heard footsteps shuffling away from the door, so he banged on it with his fist. There was no response, so he banged again. "Rich, open up! This isn't a joke, and I don't have anything to do with it!"

Behind him, Paul heard the elevator door open. Billy stepped out, his rheumy eyes watching the floor as he walked over toward Paul.

"Billy, what's going on?" Paul said.

"Mister Abler," Billy said, his right hand resting on the gun in the holster on his right hip, his eyes looking determined but a bit fearful. "I think it's time for you to go now."

"Why?"

"I just got a call from Mister Whitehead, saying you was up here causing a disturbance. We can't have disturbances in our halls. You know that."

"Billy, I live here!" Paul was standing on the balls of his feet, bouncing, waving his hands in the air. "That right there is my apartment!"

"Not anymore, Mister Abler. Mister Whitehead give me a court order just an hour ago to change the lock on the door, and so that's what I done. It's not your apartment any more."

"Billy, this is nuts!" Paul shouted.

Billy shook his head slowly and stepped forward, taking Paul's arm in his hand with a gentle but firm grip. "Now, sir, that's just how life goes. This isn't the first time somebody's been evicted here, and it won't be the last time. Now you come along with me."

"Where?"

"Out. Out the front door."

"But my stuff. I've got to get into my apartment to get my things!"

"Noon tomorrow," Billy said. "We got movers coming at noon, and it'll all be down on the dock." His voice softened. "You be here a bit early, I'll let you help them if you want. Come around eleven."

Paul jerked his arm back from Billy's grip and marched over to the elevator, pushed the button.

"You're not thinking of making any trouble for me are you, Mister Abler?" Billy said, walking over to stand behind Paul. "This ain't nothing personal. I need my job, too, you know. And I know you don't want what would happen if we had to call in the sheriff."

The elevator door opened and Paul stepped in. He turned around in the doorway so Billy couldn't enter without pushing him out of the way. "Don't worry, Billy. I'll let myself out."

## Chapter Twelve

# Despair

Paul stood on Eighth Avenue watching the afternoon traffic of cars, taxis, trucks, and pedestrians flow around him like a ceaseless river. He searched out faces, hoping to see Noah or Jim or Joshua among the people, but none of them appeared. He leaned against the black enamel steel fencing that bounded the small yard around the apartment building, and watched as two squirrels alternately chased each other up and down an old maple tree.

He called out softly, hoping none of the people walking by would hear, "Noah? Are you here?"

The squirrels didn't even turn to look at him. His only answer was the sounds of the street: car engines gunning and moaning, horns crying, a distant siren, a drunk at the newsstand across the avenue shouting at an attractive woman walking by.

He stepped out onto Eighth Avenue and turned right, walking downtown, unsure of where he was going or what he would do. He ran through his mind the short list of people he might be able to call for a place to spend the night and realized with a mild shock that none were what he would call true friends. They were all acquaintances: people he knew at work, people in his building, people he'd met while working on stories over the past years. The three close friends he'd come to know in college had all moved on; Thomas was in Atlanta, Mike in San Francisco, and Amanda had gone to Salt Lake City for a job and ended up married into a polygamous Mormon family living in a small town in southern Utah. His career had soaked up all his time, all his life, left no room for meaningful friendships.

The people from work would probably be embarrassed to see him, and of the people he'd met over the past year in his building, the only one he'd gotten to know well enough to visit each other's apartment was Rich. A lyric from an old Beatles tune about "all the lonely people" ran through his head as he looked around at the people on the street, wondering how many of them, like him, were essentially friendless in the big city.

At 27th Street he passed the Fashion Coffee Shop and, on an impulse, walked in. It was that quiet time between lunch and dinner, and there were only three tables occupied, all by students. Mary was sitting on one of the counter stools reading the newspaper. When he walked in, she looked up and smiled.

"Hi, Paul," she said.

"Hi, Mary," he replied, sitting on the stool next to her.

"This isn't your regular table."

"I'm just going to have a cup of coffee."

She got up and went behind the counter to the coffee-pot and poured him a cup, brought it over and put it in front of him. "Be right back," she said, then took a pitcher of water over to a table occupied by three young women and a shaved-head young man. On the way back she visited the other two occupied tables, went to the soft-drink dispenser and refilled a glass of cola, took it back to one of the tables. Paul watched her and wondered what her life was like when she wasn't moving plates and glasses around.

Mary returned to the stool and sat down. "Seven more minutes," she said with a glance toward the kitchen.

"Seven more minutes?" Paul said.

"Yeah, assuming Diana shows up on time. I leave in seven more minutes. I'm shot."

"Long day?"

"Fridays are always long days, because I work a full shift. Monday through Wednesdays I have classes so I only work the mornings, but I work Thursdays and Fridays from seven in the morning 'till four. There's supposed to be an hour's lunch break in there, but I prefer to catch it five minutes here and five minutes there." She tilted her head to one side in a plastic-smile gesture. "So I'm on my lunch break right now."

"What are you doing after work?" Paul said. He felt instantly embarrassed at the tired-out pickup cliché; he hadn't meant it that way. It was just a statement of curiosity. Or was it?

"Gonna walk two miles and feed my cat," she said, giving him a look that he took as curiosity. "Why?"

He shrugged, feeling suddenly warm. "I don't know. Just curious." He noticed that his armpits were suddenly sweaty, and wondered if he'd remembered to put on deodorant after his morning shower. The call from Rich had unnerved him; it was possible he'd overlooked parts of his normal routine.

"I live up near Central Park, in the Sixties," she said. "It's kinda an upscale area, but the apartment is owned by a friend of my father's, so he's giving my dad a break on the rent."

"That's nice," he said, wondering if he'd brushed his teeth.

"I mean if you want to walk me home. It's about two miles north of here, I'd guess. Almost forty blocks. Somebody once told me that every twenty blocks is a mile."

Paul realized from the tone of her voice that she was

nervous. He'd never heard her like this before; she was always so self-assured, so totally waitress-in-charge. And she'd just asked him if he'd proposed to walk her home.

"I'd love to walk you home," he said, wondering how she'd react if he asked if he could sleep on her couch. "Can I take you to dinner after you feed your cat?"

She laughed. "You getting food for me? That would be a change." She reached behind her neck, found her ponytail, pulled it over her shoulder and smoothed the hair. "Where would you like to go?"

"What's your favorite food?"

She looked at her hair for a moment as if she'd just discovered it, then tossed it back over her shoulder. "I'm vegetarian."

"Why?"

She shrugged. "I love animals. I'm not gonna eat one unless my life depends on it."

"What is love?" he said.

"Well, I feel like I'm one of them, you know?" she said. "I'm an animal. A human animal, but an animal. And I'd rather somebody didn't kill me for food, so I figure they feel the same way. And look how they struggle when they know you're going to kill them. They know, and they don't want to die. So I think love, at least in this context," she looked at the floor for a moment, "is compassion."

"What would you say if I said that God is love?"

She thought about it for a moment. "Sounds sweet enough."

"No, I mean *really*. I mean that *God is love*. That's how we experience God."

"I dunno," she said. She nodded her head toward the table with the four students. "You see that girl on the end, the one with the long red hair?"

Paul glanced over. The young woman sat with two other girls and a boy: they all had that self-conscious look of college freshmen. The redhead wore skintight black leather pants and a white lacy top that was cut so low her breasts were visible. "With her hand on the guy's leg?" Paul said.

"Yeah. They've been coming in here about four months now, this is sort of like their hangout. I've seen her fall in love three times, three different guys. And I mean, she's really falling in love with them. Head over heels. She dumped the first one, the second one dumped her; she was in here crying and talking about suicide. And now this one. But I think maybe she's just really sensitive to pheromones or she wasn't nurtured enough as a child. You know what I mean?"

"Yeah, and there could be some of that in there. It's the difference between lust and love. But love is more real, deeper."

"I love my cat," Mary said.

"Do you see God in your cat's eyes?"

"Well," Mary said, "when I look into my cat's eyes, I get the feeling sometimes that I'm looking into some kind of larger intelligence. But I'm also clear that I'm looking at a cat, who's looking back at me as a cat looking at a person. You know?"

"Exactly." He nodded at the girl at the table. "And that's the difference between you and the girl over there. She looks into a guy's eyes and feels that love feeling and thinks she's looking into God's eyes, and she doesn't realize there's a guy there, too. She's learned how to get her juice, her energy, her contact with God, by falling in love with a guy. But her mistake is she thinks that boy is the only place it is, or at least that she'll only find it by falling in love. That her only connection to God is through a boy. She doesn't realize it's inside of her, that God-ness he is making her feel. That it's God in her. She just thinks that connection to God is available through him. Of course, she wouldn't even call it a 'connection to God,' she doesn't think in those terms, but that's what's happening. She touched God once by falling in love with a boy, and now she thinks that's the only way to touch God. And it's gonna be the tragedy of her life."

Mary looked impressed. "That's so insightful."

"And I'm sure it's true. It's a Truth."

She nodded and said, "I'll look for God when I see my cat tonight." A dark-haired middle-aged woman came through the door and Mary's expression brightened. "There's Diana, only three minutes late for her shift. We can go now."

## Chapter Thirteen

# The Kings Taketh

It was the perfect end to the perfect evening, other than a few small bumps along the way.

Paul and Mary had walked the forty-some blocks to her apartment, where she'd invited him in to meet her cat, Igor. A Maine Coon Cat, Igor was easily the largest—and laziest—cat Paul had ever met. He weighed twenty-seven pounds, Mary said, and was a representative of the only breed native to North America, with the cat lore being that Maine Coons were the result of a horny and myopic northeastern bobcat encountering some unwitting farmer's domesticated cat (or, even odder, vice-versa) several hundred years ago.

In the foot-deep windowsills of her early-twentieth-century apartment building, Mary was growing a garden. Tomatoes, peppers, chard, three types of lettuce, radishes, and a dozen different medicinal and culinary herbs grew from pots, in flats, and escaped out of homemade planters. In the bathroom window was a huge squash plant, which trellised around the towel-rack and onto plumbing under the sink. "You can't trust the food you buy in the stores," Mary had told him. "It's genetically altered and laced with chemicals." So she grew about a quarter of her own food. Impressive.

They'd gone to an expensive but elegant vegetarian restaurant and had an interesting conversation in which Paul tried out several of the Wisdom School teachings he'd learned so far, checking his notepad for accuracy. Mary followed along, nodding and commenting, often reinterpreting his truths in terms of the philosophies of Carl Jung or Sigmund Freud.

Then he hit the first bump.

When he tried to pay for dinner with his credit card, the waiter came back to the table with the card cut in half on a small plate. "I'm sorry," he said, "but when we tried to get authorization on this, the credit card company asked that we cut the card in half and return it to you." He was a short, slim man, about thirty, with thinning yellow hair and pasty white skin. He continued in a nasal tone, which had been lacking earlier: "Usually if a card is overdrawn we just can't take it. They only ask us to cut them up if the card is reported stolen or has been cancelled. Do you have some other form of payment?"

Paul tried another credit card with the same result, the waiter now behaving decidedly irritated, and Paul becoming increasingly alarmed. So far, he'd managed to avoid telling Mary anything about his troubles. He was becoming so enamored of her that rather than have her think poorly of him for getting evicted, he'd decided to rent a room in a cheap hotel. He'd planned to pay for it with one of his credit cards, which he could catch up on when he found a job.

"What's going on, Paul?" Mary had asked when the waiter returned with a cut-up card for the second time.

Paul fumbled in his pockets, fishing out all his cash. The check was for sixty-three dollars and change (the price driven up by their having shared an excellent bottle of wine), and he only had forty-six dollars and two quarters on him.

"Hang on," he said to Mary. Then, to the waiter, "Can you come back in five minutes? I need to call my credit card company."

The waiter gave him a quick, skeptical appraisal and resolved the possibility of his running out on the check by saying, "You don't need to use the pay phone in the hall. There's a phone in the manager's office. Follow me."

Paul followed him into a small, cramped office next to the Ladies' room. The desk looked like a paper bomb had gone off on it, and Paul saw that most of the forms had to do with the dozens of tax-collecting and tax-assessing and tax-inventing agencies associated with the State and City of New York. The waiter waved to an old-fashioned black Bakelite phone on the desk and said, "There you are."

Paul reassembled the first credit card and dialed the 800 number on the back of it. After waiting four minutes because the phone had a rotary dial and no buttons to push to select the option of his choice, a man answered the phone with the name of the card's issuing bank.

"I've got a problem with my credit card," Paul said.

"What's the problem?" the man said, his voice carrying a pronounced Louisiana roughneck twang. Paul remembered reading in the paper about how some banks, to save money, were using prison labor. The prisoners, it seems, made about four bucks an hour and all the credit card numbers they could steal; the prisons kept ninety percent of the pay for "room and board," and the banks cut their labor costs and rolled the cost of fraud over onto the federal government. Paul wondered how many bank employees had been laid off for that little deal.

"The waiter tried to verify my credit card, and you guys told him to cut it in half."

"What's your credit card number?"

Paul read him the number. "Just for identification purposes, Mister Abler, can you please tell me your date of birth and mother's maiden name?"

Paul told him.

"And your weight, height, and hair and eye color?"

"How come you need that?"

The guy chuckled. "Just a little joke. You'd be amazed how many people think I can see them over the phone."

"Where are you?"

"California." There was a note of defensiveness in the man's voice.

"Are you a prisoner?"

"Are you unemployed and evicted?"

"Well, yeah, but what business is that of yours?"

"Me personally? None. You're a lousy credit risk." The guy chuckled, then his tone became serious. "As far as the bank is concerned, the problem is that you're a month late on your card payments and out of work, so we can't let you run up any more charges."

"How'd you find out I'm out of work?" Paul noticed the waiter lift an eyebrow and scowled at him. The man looked at the floor, but didn't leave the room.

"Lemesee," the man said, and Paul could hear a click of computer keys. "Says here that a law firm in New York City reported today that you're in default to them on thirty-seven thousand dollars in legal fees. They passed along the information about your employment and eviction as a courtesy."

"A law firm? Which one?"

The man made the noise of somebody sucking on a cigarette while Paul could hear key-clicks.

"They let you smoke there?" Paul said.

"Just tobacco," the man said, his voice soft with disappointment. "Here it is. Schneiderman, Sabatini, and Kurland, attorneys-at-law. You owe them some bucks, eh?"

"That's where my neighbor, Rich Whitehead, works. He's upset with me."

"I'll say."

"They can just report that stuff?"

"If they pay the monthly fee to subscribe to the credit bureau service."

"Even if it's wrong?"

"If it's wrong, you can request a copy of your credit history from the credit bureau, then write them a letter challenging the accuracy of the data." He sounded like he was reading from a script. "Our bank relies on information provided to it by third parties, and makes no claims as to the accuracy or . . ."

"But it's not true!" Paul shouted into the phone. The waiter smirked, but avoided eye contact.

There were a few more key-clicks, the sound of another drag on the cigarette. Then, "Scrolling down here, on the second screen, it looks here like they filed an addendum to their original report, just an hour later, saying that the listing of your owing them money was an error. They noted that the other data was valid, though." He chuckled. "They couldn't just report that you're un-employed and evicted. It wouldn't make the report, as it's not a valid complaint from them. So this guy musta concocted the phony bill, posted it with the other info added as notes, and then retracted the original so you couldn't sue them for defamation or whatever."

"I get it," Paul said.

"Bottom line, bro," the man said, "is you outa luck."

"Thanks," Paul said, an automatic reflex.

"Don't mention it."

Paul put the phone in its cradle and said to the waiter, "I need to talk to the lady."

"I'll follow you," the waiter said, wiping his hands on his apron in an exaggerated gesture.

Paul walked over to the table where Mary was sitting and reading the dessert menu as if it were an important literary work. He sat down, the waiter hovering close enough to hear the discussion.

"My credit cards are dead," he said in a low whisper.

"What happened?" Mary said. "Are you having problems?"

"Well, I had a disagreement with my next-door neighbor. Actually, he got upset with this ghost named Noah, and Noah sicced the devil on him or something like that. I never did get it straight." He caught the ex-pression on Mary's face. "I mean, anyhow, this guy who lives in the next apartment is a lawyer and he's upset with me, and so today he got me evicted and this afternoon he called the credit reporting services and said that I owed his law firm thirty-seven grand and it was overdue."

"Do you?"

"No. I don't owe them anything. But he ruined my credit, just to make some kind of macho point. And the upshot is that I don't have any credit cards that work and I don't have enough cash to pay for dinner."

She smiled and put a hand on his arm. "I always figured one day I'd have a customer stick me with a check. I never figured it would be in another restaurant, though."

"I'm really sorry . . ." Paul said, feeling a pleasant tingle from her touch mingle with his embarrassment.

"It's no problem," she said. "We should have gone Dutch treat anyway. This is the twenty-first century, after all." She lifted her purse up from the floor under her chair. "How much is the check?"

"Sixty-three dollars and change."

"So," she said, her eyes looking up to the ceiling for a moment as she did the mental math, "with a twenty percent tip, more or less, that would be about seventy-six dollars, right?"

"Sounds good to me," he said, wondering if waitresses always over-tipped.

"Do you have thirty-eight dollars?"

"Yeah," he said, thinking it would leave him—maybe—with cab fare back to her place.

She opened her purse, then a slim brown faux-suede billfold, and counted out a twenty and eighteen one-dollar bills onto the table. "I get a lot of ones," she said.

Paul put forty dollars on the table and said to the waiter, who stepped forward to scoop up and count his bounty, "Keep the change."

"Thank you, sir," the waiter said, bowing slightly at the waist, his voice conveying contempt.

Paul remembered Jim saying *the poor get no respect*, and had a depressing momentary glimpse of himself through the waiter's eyes. He was, as Susan had implied, a loser. Or at least rapidly on the road to loserdom.

Mary stood up and lifted her coat off the chair next to her. "Let's go," she said, as she pulled on the dressy red winter coat.

It was dark on the street, and they were twenty blocks from Mary's apartment. Paul shivered in his long black wool coat. "I think I have enough for cab fare," he said, "or to buy you a drink if you'd like to stop someplace." He felt utterly humiliated after the incident in the restaurant.

Mary put her hands into her pockets, her face made stark by the light and shadows from the streetlight and passing cars. "Paul, what's going on with you?" Her voice was both concerned and businesslike. "I mean, you came into the restaurant this morning and left with that homeless guy, and then you came back this afternoon when you should have been at work, and then this." She swept her right hand out of her pocket at the restaurant's door, then returned it to her pocket. "What's happened?"

"You wouldn't believe me if I told you," he said. "I'm not sure I believe it, myself."

"Try me."

"Let's walk and talk," he said, turning and beginning back uptown toward her apartment. She fell in beside him, and he thought, *ok, how would a reporter report on this story?* He decided a straight-up factual account, no side narratives or commentaries, would be best.

"You remember those things I was reading to you from my notepad over dinner?" he said.

"Yeah. Interesting stuff. I think you have the core concepts there of just about every major religion. And most of the non-destructive minor ones, too, probably. I doubt my psychology professors would agree with it all, but it makes sense to me."

"I didn't come up with that stuff myself," he said.

"I didn't think you had. I figured you'd been doing a lot of reading, or maybe in your reporting you'd found some priest or rabbi to interview, and that's what the notes were from."

"That's sort of true." They crossed a street with the light and continued. "Yesterday, I jumped in front of this truck. I wasn't thinking, it was just an impulse, I had to push this little girl out of the way so she wouldn't get hit. And something or somebody picked me up and all of a sudden I was flying through the air, and it saved her life and saved mine. And then when I got back to my apartment, there was this guy there, said his name was Noah, and he was an angel, or a ghost, or a shapeshifter, pick your culture or religion."

"Was he delusional?"

"No, I'm pretty sure he was exactly what he said he was."

And he told her the story, straight through, from his getting laid off, to saving the little girl, to meeting Noah in the doorway and going to ancient Sumeria. He covered Noah's interchanges with Rich, meeting Jim in the restaurant and Joshua in the tunnels, and Rich having him evicted and why. His decision and commitment to join in saving the world. Of the things he'd learned so far, and that there was more to come.

It took four blocks to tell in its entirety,

They walked in silence for another block, Paul dreading her response, fearing she may think him mad.

Finally she said, "That's an extraordinary story."

"As a reporter, I have to say that if somebody told me all this happened to them, I'd think they were nuts."

"Or schizophrenic, or delusional, or someone so needy for attention or love that they make up wild stories to get attention. There are less charitable sounding clinical descriptions. Like, for example, 'crazy.'" She smiled.

"I know," he said, certain that she was thinking he fit into one of those categories. "What do you think?"

She stopped in front of a well-lit store window that featured women's spring dresses in bright yellows and greens, and looked at him, face on. One eyebrow lifted slightly, and in the fluorescent light from the store window he noticed a small scar over her right eyebrow. He wondered how and when it had happened, and realized he was curious about every aspect of her life. What was her childhood like, her growing up, her adolescence, her school years? How did she relate to her parents, who were her best friends, what was her experience of first love? He looked into her eyes, and knew that he saw God looking back at him, loving him through her heart.

"I believe you," she said. She took his right hand in both of hers and held it, warming him in the chilly night air. "I'd like to meet Noah and Joshua. There's no doubt in my mind that if we don't do something soon to wake people up, the world is doomed. I'm ready to help save it."

His chest felt warm and full, the lights of the street seemed to brighten as he studied her face. The sounds of traffic receded, and he was conscious only of the sound of her breathing. "Are you serious?"

"Of course! If you aren't telling the truth, then I'll figure it out quickly enough. If you are, this sounds to me like the chance of a lifetime. It feels right to me, and as I look at your face I'm pretty sure I'm seeing somebody who doesn't lie and isn't mentally ill. Of course, the first thing they try to teach us in psychology class is not to trust our feelings but to be objective, to maintain distance from people you're trying to understand. But I don't agree with that. My intuitions have always served me well."

He ached to kiss her. Instead, he turned and continued walking up the street toward her apartment. She didn't let go of his right hand, but held it in her left hand, and he felt a thrill at walking up the street with this very attractive young woman who had so much more depth than the superficial persona of waitress and psychology student.

"I've often wondered about something in the Bible," she said, "and I think you just put it all together for me."

"What's that?"

"In Mark, Jesus told his disciples that some of them would still be alive when the kingdom of God was installed on the Earth. I always figured he just got it wrong. Now I realize he got it right."

"You mean because some of those with him realized that the kingdom was within them?"

"Yes," she said. "Those who realized that it can be right here and now, when you turn away from serving the kings of the world—mammon—and instead touch the presence and love of God within you."

"It's the story of the mystics," he said.

"What do you mean?"

"Like the Muslim, Rumi. Or the Jew, Martin Buber. Or the Catholic, Saint John of the Cross. All died already having touched, already knowing, the kingdom. Like Salome said she's done. 'Today's a good day to die.'"

"It's an amazing possibility," Mary said. "Your experiences are almost unbelievable, except the teachings make so much sense. I'd love to meet Noah."

"I can't predict when, or even if, he'll reappear," he said as they walked. She kept his hand in a firm grip. "I called for him this morning, but nothing happened. But I can take you to the tunnel to meet Joshua if you want. It would probably be best if we found Jim in the morning and had him escort us."

"He's been in the restaurant before," she said. "One time I let him use the bathroom and caught hell from the boss for it. I never knew his name."

"I think he collects cans in that part of town. It seems like the can-collectors each have their own little territories where they scavenge through the trash. I'll bet we can find him in the morning."

"That would be best," she said. "I don't want to go into the tunnels or anywhere near them at night, so that leaves tomorrow morning. But it'll have to be early, as I have a Saturday class at three."

"It's a date," Paul said, and he squeezed her hand, then let go of it, putting his hand back into his overcoat pocket. He took a deep breath and said, "I need a place to spend the night tonight. I thought I could pick up a cheap hotel room, but my credit cards are nuked, so I'm stuck. Can I sleep on your sofa?"

"Sure," she said without a moment's hesitation.

"I'm not trying to hit on you."

"I know," she said. "Or at least you're not consciously trying." He caught a smile on her face in the light of passing traffic.

"Truth is that I'm very attracted to you," he said. "But it's in a way that makes me want to take it slow and not sabotage it. It feels like God's love flowing through you to me." He put his arm around her shoulders and felt her pull close to him as they walked.

## Chapter Fourteen

# A Hard Wind

The hands of the Regulator clock on the living room wall of Mary's apartment pointed to twenty past three, and Paul stared at its pendulum for a moment, hearing the gentle tick-tock with each stroke, trying to orient himself. He was on a folded-out sofa bed, that when opened like this left little room for anything else in the room. They'd had to move the coffee table into the kitchen and push the two mismatched easy chairs into the corners.

The room had a surreal quality to it, and for a moment he wondered if he was fully awake or still dreaming. The clock continued to tick-tock, and he concluded he was awake.

He tried to figure out what it was that woke him. He'd come so completely awake that even his dreams were out of reach, faint ghostly memories that tore like wet tissue paper when he tried to reach back into memory to examine them. Something about the Holy Trinity, about Wisdom, a female elemental who said She was partner to the male Godhead. The Goddess whom Solomon wrote love poems to in The Song of Songs.

And then there had been the sound of the wind.

He shivered and looked at the window. The curtains were modern replicas of old lace, bulged out at the windowsill by leaves and stems from the pots and trays. They moved in an uncertain flutter, and Paul realized the window must be slightly opened. Mary had only one extra blanket, and he was cold.

He swung his feet out from under the sheet and blanket, dropped them to the floor, then pulled on his jeans and shrugged into his shirt. If he was going to be pulling back the curtain in Mary's apartment, he figured she may not want her neighbors to see a man in his underwear. Not to mention how cold the room had become.

He walked to the window and pulled back the curtain. Outside the window, instead of the brownstone apartment building across the street he'd seen earlier, he saw a swirl of gray and blue-black cloud, as if he were looking into the eye of a hurricane.

"What?" he said under his breath. The air seeping under the cracked-open window smelled of copper and rain and burned gunpowder. He pushed a tomato plant in a black plastic pot to one side and put a knee on the ledge, levered himself up, his other knee on the other side of the pot. He leaned forward to grip the handle at the bottom of the window, intending to push it all the way down. But it was so odd outside: the smell of the air, the swirling turbulence of the clouds. He had to know what it was. He pulled up the lower half of the window and stood on hands and knees looking out, his head and shoulders in the opening twelve floors above the street.

The swirling wind flashed with branches of lightning, and there was a sudden roar, the sound of a jet plane roaring through a deep and ancient tunnel. The air in the room exploded outward, and Paul clawed at the sides of the window, trying to keep himself from being pulled into the maelstrom. It was a futile effort; he flew through the open window, sucked into the darkness.

There was a moment of wild movement, thick with cold and pain and fear. And then he was floating in empty black space, his arms and legs out as if he were drifting just below the surface of the ocean. In the endless distance he saw stars burning with a steady, never-ending light; pinwheel galaxies slowly turned; asteroids tumbled through the black emptiness, crystalline structures glittering in distant starlight, their dark sides only discernable as shadows blotting out the stars they moved past.

Paul felt a breathless exhilaration; a feeling of déjà vu overwhelmed him. Fear drained from him, and the emptiness in his heart was replaced with a warmth that he recognized as love. He was bursting with love; it flowed through and filled every cell of his body. He thought *I wish Mary could see this*, and the loving recollection of her rippled through his body like water flowing down a mountainside. There was no sound, no smell, no taste—only light and the feelings that pulsed and flowed and pounded through him. The silence seemed to echo, and in the most vast distance he thought he could hear the faint sound of a piano slowly and softly picking out the notes to Eric Satie's *Trois Gymnopédies*. Was it a memory or real? He didn't know. Where was he and how did he get here? Somehow it didn't matter; this was so beautiful, so profound, so much larger than any puny, irrelevant human consideration of what or why or how.

And then space rang with a single word: "Behold." The voice was distinctly feminine, rich and resonant, a voice of power and authority, yet liquid with compassion. The word echoed into the vastness, then was absorbed by the stars.

"Who is that?" Paul said, his mouth making words in the airless space. He heard his own voice drift into eternity.

"Wisdom hath built Her house. She hath hewn out Her seven pillars."

"You are Wisdom?" Paul said.

A white dove flew out from behind him, a hundred

yards away, and crossed left-to-right, vanishing into the light of a nearby star, seemingly without ever noticing him. In front of him materialized a woman who bore a striking resemblance to Mary, only in her sixties or seventies. Gray hair fell around her shoulders, her eyes glittered with life and intelligence. She wore a purple robe edged in gold and held a cup in one hand. She was radiantly beautiful.

Her voice, which seemed to come from every star, every distant galaxy, and all the bits of dust around him, said, "Doth not Wisdom cry? And understanding put forth Her voice?"

"Are you here to give me my final lessons and the Greatest Spiritual Secret?" Paul said. The voice awakened in him a faint melancholy, a childhood memory, a distant time of bliss and contentment that he had long forgotten.

She said, "The Word, the Name, He shall preserve thy going out and thy coming in from this time forth, and even for evermore."

"I don't understand."

As he watched, she faded into mist and some of the stars began to change. Yellow ones bloated and became red. Red ones bloomed into blinding explosions, then turned black. White and blue ones turned yellow and red, or collapsed into blackness with a wink. Galaxies shifted in colors, rippling through violet and orange, collapsing in or spiraling out. Everything seemed to be moving away from everything else, faster and faster, as if the universe were a balloon being blown up and Paul was the only stationary thing in it. Paul realized he was watching the end of time. This was the final entropy, the era when the expansion of the universe had stretched from the Big Bang to the time when there was no more energy for expansion, no more fuel for the stars. Everything was turning to cold matter, a universe filled with stone, dust, iron, and slag.

It became darker and colder, and Paul felt the heaviness of it, the loss of heat, the last moments of creation.

As the last distant stars dimmed into red giants, their final death throes, he felt a tremendous pull, as if behind him was a huge vacuum or a magnet of unfathomable power. Matter flew past him backwards, stars and planets and dust and black holes of matter compressed so densely not even light could escape. He looked all around and saw it happening everywhere, in every direction.

The universe was collapsing back into itself.

The pace quickened, and a thunderous roar set up as planets, cold stars, black holes, unimaginable amounts of debris, collided and collapsed together, flying toward a center point, faster and faster. The point at the center became red, then yellow, then blue-white, then suddenly black, twice the size when it was blue. Paul realized it must have become so dense that its gravity would no longer allow light to leave its surface. The blackness in the center of the universe grew, fed by a billion billion stars and planets a second, swelling and trembling.

Paul hung in empty space that was truly empty, only a faint halo around the blackness at the center of the vast black emptiness revealing its existence, and that center began to shrink and become blacker and blacker. It became smaller and smaller and smaller until it seemed no larger than a distant mustard seed. For a hundred-millionth of a second it seemed to vanish, and then it exploded outward, spewing out fire and gas into all the emptiness.

Paul felt the warmth, the searing heat, heard the thunderclap and continuous roar of the explosion, as the universe again came into being. Gas clouds congealed into stars, which burst into flames, huge and small, the expansion fully underway again. Stars burned a thousand different colors, and many exploded, spewing out into space huge masses of matter, which themselves clotted together to form planets. The planets spun through space until captured by the gravity of a star, then began their busy circling dance. Atmospheres formed, rains fell, green spread across the landmasses. And soon everything was as it had been when Paul first found himself thrust into space.

"What does this mean?" he said in a hushed voice, awed by what he had just witnessed.

The woman's voice said, "If a man die, shall he live again?"

"I don't know."

Before him formed the translucent image of a woman he recognized from an old photograph as his great-grandmother. She was now a young woman in an old family bedroom, and gave birth to a girl he realized was his grandmother. He watched in horror and fascination as his great-grandmother grew old and died and was put into a wooden box and lowered into the ground. And, as if the soil was transparent, he saw the box rot and her body decompose, becoming one with the soil. The nutrients that had been her body rippled through the soil and were carried by the water into fields of wheat and vegetables. The scene changed to his mother as a young girl, eating the vegetables nourished by the body of his great-grandmother and, he realized, millions of other humans before her. He saw the faint echoing of the lives of Europeans in America in the soil, nineteenth century dress, then eighteenth century, then seventeenth, then Native Americans, nourishing the soil with the bodies of their dead elders, feeding the fruits of the nourished soil to their children. He realized all humans breathed air that had been breathed a million million times before, drank water that had run through other's kidneys a million million times since the beginning of life on Earth.

The image faded, and the woman returned. She said, "Yes," and her voice came from every particle of creation.

"Do you mean that *we shall all live again*?"

"Yes. And more."

"More?" Paul said.

"Is there any thing whereof it may be said, 'See, this is new?' It hath been already of old time, which was before us."

"Are you trying to tell me that time goes in cycles, rather than in a straight line? That there is no beginning and no end?"

"World without end, amen," she sang.

Paul took the pad and pen out of his shirt pocket and jotted down, *Time goes in cycles, rather than in a straight line; there is no beginning and no end.* "Do you have more to teach me? Noah said I would have three teachers in the Wisdom School, and I think you're the third. Or was that the Secret?"

She smiled and began a soft hum, which echoed off the distant stars; everything seemed to vibrate, like a guitar string resonating to another instrument.

The hum became words, which said, "She openeth her mouth with wisdom, and in her tongue is the law of kindness."

"Kindness?"

Before him the woman vanished and a three-dimensional image again appeared in empty space, although this time he saw streams of people running from burning buildings. As he looked closer, he realized he was seeing refugees fleeing a burning city; men and women, children, the elderly, all carrying whatever they could of their possessions, some pictures and letters and papers, others gold and jewelry, others bags of food or water. Bombs fell from the sky, soldiers fired weapons on the fleeing people, tanks spit fire and bodies exploded with blood, buildings burst into flames.

The image shifted to an ornate room, decorated in gold, white enamel, and oak. A white-haired man sat on a gold-gilt and red velvet chair large enough to be a throne. Around him were clustered other men in their forties, fifties, and sixties. Most were in military uniform, gold and silver leaves and bars and emblems. The man on the throne spoke something in a guttural language and waved his hand. In the visual echo of the hand-wave, Paul saw the refugees, the bombs, the soldiers, and he realized that this man was ordering the war; he was responsible for the pain and death Paul had seen. The man pounded his fist on the arm of his chair, and the image shook: the world trembled. *The power of evil*, Paul thought.

As if in answer to his thought, Wisdom said, "Woe to them that devise iniquity, and work evil. When the morning is light, they practice it, because it is in the power of their hand."

The scene shifted to a field hospital in the war zone. A young woman dressed in jeans and a white blouse, with a Red Cross emblem on a band of cloth tied around her upper arm, was dressing the wounds of an unconscious old woman. With each movement of her hands, each change of expression on her earnest, tragic face, the world shivered and shook as if an artillery shell had gone off. The scene shifted to a hillside street in a small European town. It was the first light of morning, and an old man dressed in a brown tweed suit walked up a deserted, rain-slicked street, hunched over as if he were intent on the pavement. With quick, efficient motions he reached down and picked up an earthworm, ran to the side of the street, and placed it on the grass. "There you are, my friend," he said. "You are the least of the least, and therefore I love you." The scene shook and trembled with each syllable; Paul could feel the intensity of it like a shock wave through his entire body. Another worm, another comforting sentence, another shock. The scene dissolved.

"The power of good," Paul said, realizing the shocks, the power, had been so much greater than that of the evil man with his army and bombs.

"Can a woman forget her sucking child, that she should not have compassion on the son of her womb?" The voice was soft and nurturing. "Yea, they may forget, yet will I not forget thee."

"Are you saying that good is more powerful than evil?"

"Unto the upright there ariseth light in the darkness: He is gracious, and full of compassion and righteous."

"Is that one of the Wisdom School teachings? That compassion is the greatest good, and good is more powerful than evil?"

"Yes," the voice said.

"Is it the Greatest Spiritual Secret of the Century?"

There was silence, and Paul felt intuitively that the woman named Wisdom had left. He took out his notebook and wrote, *Compassion is the greatest good, and good is more powerful than evil.* As he finished writing, another image began to form from mist. His heart raced as he recognized Joshua standing in front of him.

"Joshua?" Paul said. "Is that you?"

Joshua was wearing the same army pants, frayed white shirt, and threadbare cardigan V-necked sweater he had been wearing when Paul met him under the street the day before. "Yes, it is I."

"What are you doing here?"

"I'm here to give you the Secret. You will write it down, carry it out to the world, tell people in a way that will transform them, and thus begin the process of saving the world and all life."

"I am ready," Paul said, straightening his spine. "But why here?"

"This is my creation, and yours."

"You created this?"

"Yes. As did you."

"Me?"

Joshua's lips moved, but a deeper and more ancient voice came from his mouth. "And the Lord God, the Word, the Name, said, 'Behold, the man is become as one of Us, to know good and evil.'"

"One of *Us*?" Paul said. "Is that from the Bible?"

"Genesis," Joshua said simply, speaking now in his own voice again. "Do you understand now?"

Paul looked up, down, left, right, and at the distant stars ahead of him. The universe extended into infinity. He'd heard the word many times in his life—infinity—but had never understood what it really meant. "Is that the Secret?"

"In a way. Do you now understand how it all began, how it all ends, how it all begins again?"

"I understand that it does. I'm not sure I know how."

Joshua smiled, stepped forward through the emptiness, reached out and touched Paul's arm in a gesture of reassurance. At the touch, Paul again felt his heart flood with love. Tears welled in his eyes. "To know *how*," Joshua said, "you would have to touch the Mind of the Creator of the Universe. That is for another time. First, you must know the Secret, and live its truth. You must take the drivenness—the ambition and drive and enthusiasm that you were born with and that you have wasted in the world of commerce—and transform it to a higher work. Can you do that?"

"Yes, of course!" Paul said. He'd always *wanted* to be a reporter, but now he *knew* who and what he really was. Every moment of his life up to this had been a preparation for his true life's work. "I am ready."

"When you know the Secret, you will find that all things are possible unto you, and that the future of the planet, of all life, is in *your* hands and the hands of those you share it with."

"And the Secret is?"

"All sprang from the One. All returns to the One. You and I are of the One, and will all dissolve back into the One." He paused and brushed his hand across Paul's face. "Come close."

Paul stepped forward and Joshua breathed on him, his mouth opened in an O. Paul smelled jasmine and frankincense and sandalwood.

Then Joshua said, "My son, the Greatest Spiritual Secret of the Century, of every Century, is '*We Are All One.*'"

For a long moment there was stillness through all creation, then Joshua slowly dissolved into the emptiness.

Paul searched the stars, the depths of empty space, wondering what was next. He felt himself supported, as if he were sitting in an easy chair with his feet up on a footstool. As the sensation became stronger, he noticed his body assuming a reclining posture, and then, in a blink, he was in the tunnel under New York, around the fire, with Joshua and the others. The air was cool, and in the distance he heard a cat meow. He felt through the ground beneath his recliner chair the far distant rumble of a subway train. The distant tunnels, which during the day had shown cracks of light from above, now were a black emptiness.

Juan was stirring a pot of stew again, although this food smelled of sage, basil, green onions, and thyme, instead of curry. This wasn't a memory: it was *now*, Paul thought.

He blinked and looked around. Everybody was looking at him, as if he'd just appeared in the old velour recliner, which he assumed he had. "What time is it?" he said.

"Around three in the morning," Salome said. "Maybe a little after."

"You're all up and awake?" Paul said.

"Joshua said you'd be visiting," Jim said.

Joshua smiled at Paul, as if they shared a secret.

"Was he gone?" Paul said to Jim, pointing at Joshua.

"No, he's been here all day," Jim said, matter-of-factly. "You're the one who just appeared." He smiled broadly.

Joshua leaned forward in his white plastic lawn-chair and said, "I imagine you have a question? Maybe something you're not quite sure of?"

Paul said, "That's the understatement of the century." He sat up a bit straighter and stretched his back and legs, organizing his thoughts. "I get it that 'We are all one' makes sense in the world of physics or metaphysics, but what does it mean in the practical world of everyday life? How can a person live this?"

"How would you live it?" Joshua said.

"Well," Paul said, "first of all, in my everyday life, I guess it would mean that I couldn't continue to just get along and go along, to feed the machine of the multinational corporations and the kings and despots of the world, to be a wage slave. I'd want to find a way to make a living that wasn't toxic to the Earth, to other humans, to all life."

"That's one possible 'doing' part," Joshua said, his tone implying there was more.

"Should I join a movement like Greenpeace or something?"

Joshua smiled. "That is the greatest challenge, Paul, for every awakened human. What to do? The answer is that there isn't one answer: there are *six billion* answers, the number of humans on Earth today. Each person must search her or his life, looking for those moments when she was most passionate about something, when he heard clearly the message of oneness—perhaps in another context, said another way—and totally understood it, if even only for a moment. In that memory, that place, you will find what you must do. For some people it may mean joining a cause, like you mentioned. For others it will mean they continue to do exactly what they're doing now, only do it with an awakened consciousness so that their work and their contacts with others become infused with oneness. For others it will mean stepping into a world of outreach or perhaps even stepping back from the world for a while to recharge themselves spiritually and thus raise the vibration of all humans and all life."

"So my way . . ."

"Is your way," Joshua said. "Only you know that, and it may take you a minute to realize it, or maybe days or weeks or months. But you will know, and when you know you will step forward into a new life with a power and love and meaning greater than any you have ever known before."

"Should I join you? Come live in the tunnel?"

Joshua shrugged. "Examine your life, all the way back to your childhood, and look and listen for the times when you *knew* what to do. There you will find the clues as to what you must do next, whether it is to join us for a while and chronicle our message, or go back to the newspapers, or to do something else altogether."

"Okay," Paul said. "I get it that if enough people took right action then governments could change, corporations could be transformed, neighborhoods revitalized, families healed, the world saved. But how does that come from knowing that 'we are all one'? I'm still not sure of the connection."

Joshua nodded and looked at Salome, as if asking her to answer the question. She leaned forward in the other recliner chair in the circle, dropping her feet to the ground as the back of the chair creaked forward.

"First I gotta tell you," she said, "it don't mean everybody in the world lives the same way, or there's some one perfect religion or lifestyle or anything like that. You understand? No one world or one way."

"Yeah," said Paul, realizing that she was the perfect person to know the truth of that.

"I mean, diversity is crucial," she said. "Like in any ecosystem, it's the same with humans. We've gotta protect diversity. This notion that America is a great melting pot, for example, and that everything would be great if only the rest of the world would live just like American middle-class white folks is wrong. It's the velvet glove over the iron fist of a dominating culture. It profits the multinational corporations if everybody has the same values and consuming habits, if everybody likes the same soft drink and jeans and TV shows, but it's not good for humanity or the world."

"I understand," Paul said. "But if it's important that we have different and diverse tribes and clans and cultures and religions, then how are we 'all one'?"

She smiled. "You know, when Jesus was talking with his friends—who included a couple of women . . ."

"Mary Magdalene and Salome?" Paul said, realizing that every person around the circle carried the modern version of a Biblical name. *Coincidence*? he wondered.

"Yeah," Salome said. "And Mary, and Joanne, and others. Although somehow they usually get overlooked or ignored." Her lips drew together as if she'd tasted something bitter, then relaxed. She continued, "But there was a story. Maybe you remember it, a parable, that Jesus laid on his friends. He talked about how a bunch of folks came to a king and said they wanted to hang out with him. You remember?"

"I'm not sure," Paul said.

She glanced over at Jim. "You know the story, Jim?"

"Sure," he said. "You want me to tell it?

"Please," Salome said.

"Well," Jim said to Paul, "in the story, this divine king—the Son of Man—invited some folks to hang out with him in heaven. He told them they were invited because when he was hungry they'd fed him, when he was thirsty they'd given him something to drink, when he was a stranger they'd taken him in and helped him out, when he was naked they gave him clothes, when he was sick they visited him, and when he was in prison they came to see how he was doing."

Jim looked at the I-beams dancing in the flickering

light from the fire for a moment, as if checking to see that he had the list right.

Paul said, "I think I remember this. It's about doing unto others, right?"

"More like, 'there's no such thing as *others*,'" Jim said. "We really are all one! The way you treat me, you treat the whole world, and vice-versa. High and low, king and servant, man and God, even, I think, human and all other life. It's why I pick up worms on the sidewalk and put them back in the grass. 'Cuz they're part of me, too, if I'm part of all life."

"The story, Jim?" Salome said.

"Oh, yeah," Jim said. "So in that story, these folks told this king they didn't recall having done any of that stuff—in fact they hadn't even known he'd been hungry, or homeless, or in prison, or any of it. They'd helped out other folks, for sure, but not him. Heck, they hadn't even seen him around. So how, they asked him, could they be the ones who'd helped him out when he'd been in trouble that they didn't even know about?"

"And?" Paul said, listening carefully.

Jim stared at the ceiling for a moment and said, "Lemme get this right, I mean exactly right, because it's one of the best 'we are all one' statements in history." He brought his gaze back down to Paul with an expression of steeled certainty and continued: "This's it. He said to them, 'Verily I say unto you, whatever you have

228

done unto one of the least of these my brethren, you have done it unto me.'"

The crash shook Paul awake.

He sat up straight on the sofa bed, disoriented.

What was happening? The vision had disappeared; instead of the tunnels, he was surrounded by Mary's living room. Plaster walls replaced the echoing vastness of space; the sound of a radiator creaking, traffic on the street outside, a rustling from the bedroom replaced the thundering silence.

The door to Mary's bedroom opened and she stood in the doorway, wearing a robin's-egg blue flannel nightshirt that came down to her knees. Her hair hung over the front of her left shoulder. "That's a sound I don't usually hear in the winter," she said.

"What sound?" Paul said, hearing his pulse in his ears.

"That window slamming shut. Sometimes in the summer it'll do it, especially if there's a rapid change in humidity. If you pull it all the way up, it just sticks there, except sometimes when it gets real dry, and then it crashes down."

"The window?"

"Yeah. That one," she pointed to the window four feet beyond the foot of his bed. "When it was originally built there were lead weights inside the casement and ropes that went from them to the lower windowpane. You can see the pulleys are still there, up near the top. But the ropes rotted away long ago."

She walked over to the window and pulled the lace curtain back, looked at the glass and her plants. "Everything seems okay. Did you open the window? Are you too warm?"

"I don't know," Paul said, grappling with reality. Mary's voice was Wisdom at a younger age: it brought back the dream in detail. "I may have. I dreamed I did."

Igor came out of Mary's room with a "Meow?" He walked over to the sofa-bed with the leisurely gait only cats can affect, and hopped up into Paul's lap.

"You dreamed you opened the window?" Mary said, walking over to the bed to stroke Igor's head. The cat purred in response.

Paul looked at the clock. Three twenty-five. "Yeah, I guess so. I don't know what to make of it."

She sat on the bed next to him. He could smell her body, warm and female, thick with the musk of humanness. "Are you ok?"

He leaned back onto the rear cushions of the sofa and said, "Yeah, I'm fine. I just had the most incredible dream. Can I tell you about it?"

She pulled her feet off the floor and crossed her legs on the bed, pushing the nightshirt down between them. "Sure. I'd love to hear it."

## Chapter Fifteen

# A Wheel Within a Wheel

Paul woke to the feeling of Mary's breath on the side of his neck. In a rush he remembered the evening, his telling her about the dream, their discussion about its meaning. She'd spent two years immersed in Carl Jung's work and writings, and had several different ideas about what his dream may mean. After an hour of discussion, drawing intellectually, emotionally, and physically closer and closer, he'd finally pulled her to him and they'd kissed. Later, she crawled under the blanket, saying, "This is just to keep warm," and he'd murmured agreement. They'd looked into each others' eyes and it was the gentlest *no* either had ever given or received. They fell asleep in each other's arms, Igor above the blanket and on top of Mary's hip, the three feeling totally One.

He disengaged from her and got out of bed, walked

around and pulled his jeans on over his underwear, and went to the bathroom. When he came out, the bed was empty, the door to her room was closed, and he could hear her opening drawers. The clock on the wall ticked its way through nine A.M.

"Good morning!" he called through the door.

"Good morning, Paul," she said. She pulled the door open, still wearing her nightshirt, a pile of clothes in her hand. "I'll take the first shower, okay? That way I can dry my hair while you're in there."

"Fine with me."

As she headed into the bathroom, he began to put the sofa bed back together and rearrange the room the way it had been when he'd arrived the night before.

They made breakfast together; he toasted the bread and she poached the eggs. A grapefruit and a pot of green tea rounded out the meal, that they ate together at the two-person kitchen table. Igor was so affectionate that he was distracting until Mary opened a can of cat food. Sated, he retired to the sofa to clean himself while they ate and talked.

"My class today is abnormal psychology," she said with a broad smile. "Maybe I should bring up your experiences the past two days. Thursday you meet an angel, Friday you meet a holy man, and in the early hours of Saturday morning you hang out in outer space with what sounds an awful lot like the Holy

Ghost or the archetypal goddess. And they're all telling you that you now have to save the world."

"They'd say we're both abnormal," Paul said with a laugh. "Me for saying it, and you for taking me seriously." It was a bright, sunny morning and the light streamed in the tall kitchen window, making the yellow of his egg's yolk and the red of the Tabasco he'd put over it particularly vivid. Outside the window, the city teemed with life, cars honked and screeched, a distant explosion sounded like a gunshot but, Paul knew, was probably just a firecracker. The normal sounds of the city seemed so much more alive to him, so much more real and present.

Mary cut her egg and toast carefully, as if it were a vitally important work. She put the bite in her mouth and chewed it, looking at him with a steady gaze. He felt like he was looking into the eyes of somebody he'd shared lifetimes with. Cycles within cycles, as Wisdom had taught him. Wheels within wheels. *How many times have we met before?* Paul wondered, meeting her gaze as he chewed his food.

He finished his bite and said, "I have this very strange feeling about you. Like I've known you forever."

"Maybe you have," she said. "I've always been interested in metaphysics and religion, but I guess I never took it very seriously. Always figured it was the mind at work, somehow."

"Or vice-versa. What if the mind is a reflection of something much larger at work?"

"Like?"

"Like everything. If we are all one, I mean *really* we are all one, then there is nothing separating us. It's only a dream, the idea that we're separate beings. It's not that we have consciousness, it's that we are *expressing* consciousness, the mind of the universe, of all creation, shining feebly out through our eyes, echoing in our words, shimmering in our deeds. Like the cup of water separate from the ocean, thinking it's only a cup of water."

She looked in his eyes. "The ocean knows the water in the cup, but the water in the cup has no idea how vast the ocean is."

"Or that other cups of water are also the ocean," he said, feeling a deep connection to her.

"If you really extend it out," she said, "then a lot of things that seem like mysteries start to make sense. The things that Jesus said about treating others like they were us, about not even going to church until you let go of even the smallest grudge against anybody, even his non-violent opposition to the Roman dominators, saying that evil must not be resisted with evil."

"And," Paul added, "it would mean that there is no time, no space: they're just ideas in the living mind of the universe, of God. It's all one, it's all interconnected.

It all sprang from love, and it all dissolves back into love. Time isn't a straight line, it's a continuous circle, like the Native Americans say. They didn't fear death as frantically as we do because they knew it was just one part of the circle, the wheel that spins forever. It's why Wisdom said her tongue was the law of kindness, because kindness is how the One loves itself. I mean, it's so easy to say, 'We are all one,' but when you really think about it, all the implications, you discover it's incredibly deep. It's at the original mystical core of every religion, of all the ancient teachings, and of all the indigenous cultures' ways of life, their understandings of life. It shines a light on all the different religions, and lets you sort out the truth in the world's scriptures from the stuff that's just one group trying to play control games over another group."

She leaned forward on her elbow and said, "The Jews say a prayer, 'Hear O Israel, the Lord our God, the Lord is one.' I wonder how many realize that it could mean so much more than just, 'There is one deity and He is ours'? That in the deepest sense it could mean that *all* is one?"

"I suspect the Jewish mystics understand that," Paul said, "just like the Christian mystics understand the same thing when they read Jesus' words that, 'I and my Father are one' or, 'Love one another as I have loved you,' or 'Is it not written in your law, "I said, Ye are gods?"' It literally means that each of us is a part of God looking at Himself."

"Or Herself," Mary said, smiling broadly.

"It would be greater even that either of those," Paul said. "Beyond gender, beyond our ability to conceive with just our thinking mind. We could only know it with our hearts."

"In love," she said in a soft voice.

"Yes," he said, feeling his heart race. "Completely and totally in love."

She looked out the window. "I think if what's happened to you is real, I want to be a part of it. It's why I went into psychology, after all. I figured it was the best way for me to save the world, one person at a time."

He struggled with his emotions. Finally he blurted out, "I'd love to have you with me."

She looked embarrassed, as if she'd said too much, too fast. "What are your plans?" she asked, changing the subject.

"Take you down to meet Joshua, first off," he said. "Then, while you're at class, I've gotta get down to the loading dock at my apartment building and arrange to get my stuff stored until I can find a place to live. After that, I'm going to pick up a paper and make a few calls looking for a job. And I may call my older brother and ask if I can borrow some money for a while. He lives in Denver. Runs a bookstore. Anyhow, I've gotta find a place to live and get a job before I can think of anything else. I appreciate your letting me use the couch last night, but don't want to abuse your hospitality."

She reached across the table and put her hand on his. "You're really welcome to stay here a few days, if you want."

"I appreciate that," he said, measuring his words. He wanted to say that he'd love to move in with her, to live with her, that he even had fantasies about marrying her. But they'd had one sex-free evening together, and he didn't want to risk blowing up the relationship by moving it along too fast.

"I mean on the couch," she added, as if she'd read his mind.

"I know," he said, putting his free hand on hers. There was a moment, a beat of almost unbearable intimacy, and then they both pulled their hands back and returned to breakfast.

An hour later, just short of noon, they walked down Madison Avenue, having already decided to walk cross-town on 34th Street; there was a bookstore there where Mary wanted to stop. At 42nd Street, she gestured to the right and mentioned that Times Square was just a few blocks over, turning them to a discussion of the changing nature of the city over the years.

At 41st Street, they stopped for the light at the same intersection where three days before Paul had pushed the little girl out of the way. "This is where it all started," Paul said, turning to Mary.

She wasn't there.

But there was the little girl he'd rescued, sobbing in the arms of her mother. And the balding man who'd told him he'd leaped across the street.

The world tilted on its side.

## Chapter Sixteen

# Home Again

Paul looked up at the crowd of people standing around him, his head aching with a bright, sharp throb. He was lying on his back on the street, the top of his head resting against the curb. He tilted his head down and looked at his hands; they were scuffed and bleeding, and the side of his face felt like it had been hit with a belt sander. The woman was crying, holding her daughter, and the man in the tan coat leaned over Paul, holding his wrist as if he were taking his pulse.

"You okay, son?" the man said.

"I don't know," Paul said. His voice sounded odd in his head, as if he were wearing headphones and his voice had been somehow amplified. He shook his head to try to clear the thickness he felt, but the motion shot a blinding flash of pain through his temples.

"Easy, son," the man said. "Somebody called 911

and there's an ambulance on its way. Let me see your eyes." He put his face directly in front of Paul's, and looked at his eyes. "Even dilation. That's a good sign. Means you probably don't have a concussion, at least not in the back of your head."

"Are you a doctor?"

"I was a medic in the Army," the guy said. "In Vietnam."

"What happened?"

The woman leaned over him and said, "You're a hero. You saved my daughter's life."

"What?"

"You pushed her out of the way, and the truck hit you," she said. "Thank God you're still alive."

"The truck hit me?"

"Knocked you ten feet through the air," the man said. "You're lucky. It could have run over you."

Paul noticed the sound of a siren, and thought of all the times he'd watched ambulances try to struggle their way through the traffic of Manhattan, sirens screaming, ignored by cars and taxis unless they opened an opportunity to sneak through a red light.

"Look out, get back!" came a loud voice, and Paul turned to see a police officer push his way through the crowd. "How are you?" he said.

"His pulse is regular and his pupils are both the same size," the man in the tan coat said. "His eyes track, and he seems coherent. We haven't moved him. I was a medic in Vietnam."

"Thanks," the cop said, dropping to one knee and looking into Paul's face. "What's your name?"

"Paul Abler." He started to sit up, but the cop put his hand on his chest and said, "Stay there until the ambulance gets here. Where do you live?"

"I don't know yet," Paul said. "I mean . . ."

"Do you know where you are?"

"New York . . ."

"What day is it?"

"Saturday."

The cop shot the man a worried glance, looked back at Paul. "What month?"

"February."

He looked up and said to the man in the tan coat, "Where's the truck that hit him?"

The man said, "Over there," and pointed in a direction Paul couldn't follow without sitting up.

The cop stood up. "Keep an eye on him and don't let him get up until the EMT says it's ok."

"Got it, sir," the man said, sitting on the curb next to Paul's head. The cop walked over to interview the driver.

"I think I'm okay," Paul said. "I mean my head hurts, and I'm skinned up, but I think I'm ok."

"Just relax," the man said.

"Where's Mary?"

"Who?"

"The woman who was with me. Mary Robbins."

The man shook his head. "There was nobody I saw with you. If she was here, she's gone now."

Paul lifted his right knee and felt a deep bruising pain in his hip. He realized his right shoulder and arm felt similarly injured.

"Take it easy, son," the man said, the sound of a nearby siren winding down behind him.

Paul let his leg fall back to the pavement. "I feel bruised but don't feel like anything's broken."

"You're in shock," the man said. "You don't even know what day it is. Here're the EMTs."

Billy gave him a wide-eyed look as he limped into the fluorescent-lit lobby of his apartment building. "You look like you been run over by a truck."

"I was," Paul said with a wry grin.

"Seriously?"

"Yeah. Well, hit, anyway," Paul said as he walked toward the elevators. "Spent the afternoon in the hospital getting x-rays and all."

Billy shook his head. "I'm sorry to hear that. I ever tell you about the time I broke my back skydiving?"

"Yeah, you have," Paul said as the elevator door opened.

"You'll heal," Billy said.

"Physically," Paul said as the doors closed. "I'll heal physically."

Rich answered the door of his apartment wearing a blue terrycloth robe.

"You have company?" Paul said.

"What happened to you?" Rich said. "Mugged?"

"Hit by a truck," Paul said.

"Then come right in," Rich said, pulling the door open. "You get hit by a truck in this city, you can make a fortune. And I get half!"

Paul stepped into the familiarity of Rich's apartment. Black leather, glass, and chrome; it smelled of pot and shampoo and leather. Signed Dali prints adorned the walls, and the carpet was a startling pure eggshell white. A big-screen TV dominated the far corner, near the window out over the balcony, and in a chair next to it sat a stunning blonde woman, wearing only a silk bathrobe with a dragon embroidered down one side. Her hair was damp, and she looked like she was in her very early twenties.

She looked Paul up and down quick, and turned on a professional smile, all teeth and eyes, and said, "Hi, I'm Cheryl."

"Hi, I'm Paul." He turned to Rich. "I really don't want to interrupt."

"It's okay, Paul," Rich said, his voice that of an old friend or a wise older brother. "I took the afternoon off work and we don't have to get dressed for another half-hour. Vodka tonic?"

"Sure," Paul said.

"They give you any pain pills at the hospital?" Rich said as he mixed the drink at a fold-down bar next to the TV. "I wouldn't want you dying over a drink with pills. Your heirs would sue me, and I'd lose all the money I'll make suing this trucking company for you."

"Just Tylenol," Paul said.

"Then only one drink," Rich said. "That stuff is incredibly bad for the liver when you mix it with alcohol." He handed a cold glass to Paul. "Now, tell me about the truck? Was it a big company or some local jerk with no insurance?"

"Actually, that's not what I wanted to talk to you about," Paul said. "I ran out in front of him, he had a green light, so it wasn't his fault."

"That doesn't matter," Rich said. "Just the threat of a suit and they'll settle for low six figures to avoid the legal costs of winning. You want a couple hundred grand?"

Paul felt uncomfortable with the way the conversation was going. Oddly, yesterday he would have jumped at the opportunity. The money could finance his career. But now it seemed, somehow, less important. Even distasteful. Maybe it was just the shock of the accident, he thought. Maybe he'd feel differently tomorrow. "Let's put that on the table for a later discussion. I came by because I'm looking for a job and thought maybe you'd know of any opportunities."

"What happened to your job with the *Trib*?"

"Layoff. I upset the wrong people, so my name was on the list when it came time to cut the workforce and up the month's profit."

Rich nodded sagely. "There's a lot of that going around. My dad says in his time, a company laid off people it meant they were going out of business. Bosses who did it were considered criminals. Now people are totally disposable."

"And I got disposed of. Rich, I'm a very good writer, and I know how to dig for information. Do you think . . ."

Rich held up his hand. "Just a second, buddy." He picked up a wireless phone and sat in a leather chair next to the sofa. "Sit down," he said to Paul as he dialed the phone. Paul sat on the sofa.

"Bob!" he said into the phone in a hale and hearty voice. "It's Rich! How ya doin'?

"Yeah, me too. Anyhow, Bob, you know that case you hired that screwup PI for? The guy couldn't write up his notes worth a damn?

"Well, I got a guy here who can do the job and do it right. I think we can use him in a big way. You know how hard it is to find somebody who's both a good investigator and a good writer, and the writing of the report is what makes or breaks the case in court, 'cepting, of course, your brilliant oratory. Well, this guy was a reporter for the *Trib*, journalism school graduate, the whole enchilada, and I know him personally; he's a good friend. He's hungry, you know what I mean? A man headed for the top. And I was telling him what a hell of a time we're having finding good investigators. That all these PIs we've hired are good at keyhole peeping and Dumpster diving, but on a corporate case they're lost; they don't know how to walk the walk, how to handle an executive or a boardroom. And no matter what they do they can't write up anything that would persuade a jury to give an old lady her cat back. You know what I mean?

"Well, I think he's thinking that he'd like a little more excitement and a lot more money than the *Trib* pays, you know what I mean? I think I could get him now. He's like in one of those trying-to-figure-out-what-to-do places, you know what I mean? If we put him on salary, it'd cost us a quarter of what we're paying to these PI firms, and we'll get twice the quality and full-time work."

Rich put his hand over the microphone and said to Paul, "How much were you making at the *Trib*?"

"Thirty-seven thousand a year."

Rich winced. "That stinks!" He took his hand off the microphone. "Listen, Bob, I happen to know for a fact that if we offer him ninety a year plus benefits, I can have him in the office ready to hit the ground running tomorrow morning. I can pull ten percent of that out of my budget if you need, but you run the investigations show. This guy's a friend, but more important, he'll make us all stars, you know what I mean? I mean, he's really good, a trained investigative reporter, and he has the instincts of a pit bull."

Paul caught his mouth hanging open and closed it. He noticed Cheryl had a broad smile on her face. He picked up the drink and took a big sip, the ice cubes banging against his front teeth. The ache in his hip was subsiding.

"Yeah, ok, I'll bring him in. If you don't want him, we'll just pay him five hundred for the day, call it a consulting fee, 'cuz he's gonna have to skip work tomorrow to come in for the interview, you know what I mean? I mean, tomorrow's Friday, it's a business day. If you like him, maybe there's even stuff he can do over the weekend. Yeah, I agree. This is *exactly* what we needed."

Rich hung up the phone, glanced at Cheryl with a look of triumph, and said to Paul, "That work for you?"

"Yeah!" Paul said. "Just like that?"

"Most likely," Rich said. "We really are having a problem, and the really good guys get two hundred an hour. That's four hundred grand a year, but of course most of it is going to the PI agency; they're probably getting one fifty, maybe two hundred grand a year. You can make that easily by the end of this year if you're as good as I said you are."

"What's the job?"

"Essentially, corporate espionage. You get inside companies and figure out where the dirt is hidden. It's pretty much the same thing as you did to that company in London you told me about last week."

"That was the story that got me canned."

"I warned you. With newspapers these days, to get along, you gotta go along."

"So I discovered."

Rich stood up and Paul realized he was being dismissed. He stood up and started toward the door, as Rich intercepted him, a hand on his shoulder. "Meet me in the hall tomorrow morning at eight-thirty. I'll take you up there with me."

"Will do," Paul said.

"And are you sure you weren't injured in that accident? You got a hospital report?"

"I was knocked out a few minutes, at the most," Paul said. "Had some pretty wild dreams, and my hip is purple and yellow, but I'm ok."

"Get somebody to take some Polaroids of the injured area," Rich said. "You lose anything? Anybody go through your pockets while you were out? Something fall out and somebody walks away with it? That happens all the time to accident victims."

"Just my notebook," Paul said. "It's not like I was a diamond courier or something."

"Still, you were injured. Get the pictures. I guarantee you, just one letter over my letterhead and they'll be begging you to take some money. Even if it's forty, fifty grand, it's better than nothing.

"I'll think about it," Paul said.

"Hey, don't go all self-righteous on me, bud. This is New York City. When a bus hits a car or a light pole, people run to get *onto* the bus, so they can fall to the floor holding their necks."

"I know, Rich."

"Get along, go along, make a pile of money."

Paul pulled the door open and stepped into the hall. "Got it."

"Good." The door closed behind him. Paul looked at the door to his apartment for a moment, thought about TV or sleep or even a good book, but instead turned, walked to the elevator, and pushed the *down* button.

As he entered the restaurant, Mary walked briskly in front of him, carrying a pot of coffee from one table to another. She glanced at him, did a double take when she saw the scratches on the side of his face, and said, "Get in a fight?"

"With a truck, up on Madison Avenue," he said to her receding back, his heart racing. She threw a smile over her shoulder, then continued on her way. The place was less than half full, the dinner rush not having yet started in full force.

His favorite table by the window was empty, so he sat down and put his coat over the chair next to him. Out on the street, a steady stream of people moved purposefully in the cold, late afternoon air. He focused on them, trying to anchor himself in the reality of the moment so he could let go of his dream of Mary, of sleeping beside her, of the smell of her hair, the sound of her night-voice, the touch of her lips. She came to the table, a pad now in her hand, and said, "Late lunch or early dinner?"

"Both, I guess. How have you been?"

She brushed a loose strand of hair off her forehead. "Okay. Studying like crazy." She was wearing jeans and a brown tee-shirt with Geronimo on the front over the words "No Fear."

"Abnormal psych?"

She tilted her head slightly, her eyebrows pulled together. "I told you already?"

"Just a guess," he said.

"There's something weird," she said, then hesitated.

"Weird?"

"I'll have to get my purse. It's in the back." She turned around and walked off toward the kitchen. Paul watched her with a glow in his chest and turbulence in his stomach. It had seemed so real. He wanted her, and he wanted the mission Joshua had given him. Moving from one big corporation to another, even for vastly more money, would never give him the sense of mission and purpose he'd known when he'd decided to take on Joshua's work, to spread the word, *to save the world.* Yet now . . .

Mary came back from the kitchen, a small green spiral-bound notepad in her hand. It was similar to the one Paul used to take notes when he was working a story. She said something to Diana, the other waitress, and then pulled out the chair opposite his and sat down. Her face had a serious expression, as if she were worried or embarrassed.

"I don't know how to say this, because it's gonna sound crazy . . ." she said, putting the notepad on the table between them, her voice trailing off as Paul reached for it.

Paul recognized it as his from the little doodle on the corner of the cover, an aimless drawing he'd done a week earlier while waiting, on hold, in his office at the *Trib.* He heard Wisdom in Mary's voice, and willed his hands to not tremble as he lifted the cover of the pad and saw written in his own handwriting on the first page, *The teachings of the Wisdom School . . .*

Mary said, "It's got your name on the back cover." She turned it over, and there was *Paul Abler* and his phone number at the *Trib* printed in his neat block lettering.

He dropped the cover as if it were hot and put his hands together on the table. "Did you read any of it?"

She looked down at her hands on the table and put her fingers together as if in prayer. "Yes. I know it was wrong of me, but I did." She looked up at him. "It's remarkable what you've written there. Reading it gave me an odd sense of déjà vu. Like it's all about things that I once knew but then forgot . . . like I was born knowing it but as I grew up I had to push it aside." She reached out and put a fingertip on the back of his hand, sending a thrill through him. "I didn't realize you had an interest in these kinds of things."

"I've taken on a job," he said, not needing to explain it further. She pulled back her hand and he felt a sense of loss. He added, "You said something would sound crazy?"

"How I got it," she said. "I found this in my apartment this morning. It was half under the sofa, half out. "I have no idea how it got there. Honest to God, I didn't find it here and take it home or anything like that. I'm sure I didn't. It was just *there*."

"With your cat Igor?"

Her eyes got wide, then narrow. "You been stalking me or something? Is this some kind of a joke?" She sat up straighter in the chair. "Did you break into my apartment and leave this?"

"No, not at all," Paul stammered. "Probably I left it here, you picked it up and put it in your pocket without thinking about it, and it fell out there." He glanced around, struggling to find the right words to say to reassure her; whenever he lied he always felt like everybody knew it instantly. Among the bustling people outside the window, he recognized the homeless man digging through the trash at the corner of Eighth Avenue. "Jim!" he said out loud.

Mary looked out the window and said, "The homeless guy?"

"Yeah, I think I know him."

"He's a regular," she said, her tone sad. "I almost got fired for letting him use the bathroom once."

"I know," Paul said. He stood up. "Come with me."

She stood up, a confused and concerned expression on her face. "What is going on here?"

"We've got to talk to Jim."

"Are you nuts?"

"Maybe." He took her arm gently, holding her. "Everything is okay and I'm not a stalker or anything like that. But I think Jim may know how that notebook ended up in your apartment."

She glanced over at Diana, who was moving at double-speed to take care of both of their tables. "I have to get back to work. Really I do. There's only a half-hour left on my shift, and I can't use it to goof off if I want to keep my job. You have your notebook, and when you figure out how it got in my apartment, please let me know."

She pulled away from his grip and marched over to a table on the other side of the room, order pad at the ready.

Paul, at a loss for words, watched her go, then grabbed his notebook, spun around, and ran out the door, leaving his coat behind on the chair. Jim was digging through a near-full garbage can, a round mesh contraption chained to the streetlight post, dropping cans into a burlap sack.

"Jim?" Paul said.

The man stopped, straightened up, and turned to look at Paul. "Do I know you?" he said.

"Do you know Joshua?"

Jim smiled wide. "Of course."

"And Matt, and Pete, and Salome, and Mark, and Juan?"

"You're talking about my family," Jim said. He tilted his head an inch to the right. "Who are you, nice clothes but looking like you just left a dogfight?"

"Joshua can heal people, right?"

"Who *are* you?"

"I'm Paul, and I know Joshua from another time and place."

"And that time and place is?"

Paul searched about his mind for a moment, then said, "'Wisdom has built Her house, and has hewn Her seven pillars.'"

Jim stepped back and looked Paul up and down. "He told us to expect you. But you're not what I expected."

"I'm not what *I* expected," Paul said. "Can you take me to see Joshua? In the tunnels?"

Jim nodded slowly. "It's a work that's easy to get into, but nearly impossible to leave."

"Why?"

"Would you leave The One?"

"Never," Paul said with conviction.

"But you gotta know we ain't some kind of cult. Joshua is just another person, just like you and me. He's right up front about that. He says that if anybody tells you they got some secret teaching from some invisible or hidden being or some group of secret teachers, then you should run in the other direction cause that's the game the phonies always run to get people to follow them, bow to them, be impressed by them. Jesus was totally transparent, his life was right out there for everybody to see. He answered everybody's questions, had no secrets and no secret teachers. Same with Moses, Mohammed, Buddha, all of them. If you think this is one of them cults where only one guy knows who or where some secret teachers are, or what some secret truths are, then you're in for a disappointment."

"I understand," Paul said. "The One isn't Joshua. It's

everything, everybody. You, me, and," he pointed to a businessman crossing with the light, "that guy there. Although he may not yet realize it."

Jim nodded. "Yeah, you understand. You ready to go now?"

Paul looked down at his once-pressed jeans and white shirt, over at his apartment building two blocks up the street, back at the restaurant. The world is in flames and crisis, he thought, and a spiritual disconnection is at its core. There are people walking around right here and now with the answers.

He took a deep breath, smelling auto exhaust, fresh-baked bread, and the cigarette smoke from a passer-by. The air chilled him without his coat. He only had about fifty dollars in his pocket. Yet he knew he had completed the first part of his training.

Was he ready to join Joshua in taking the Secret to the world? To give the energy of his life over to saving the world?

He imagined himself receiving the Pulitzer Prize and realized it was irrelevant to him now. Nothing less than the survival of life itself, of every human and every other living thing on Earth, was at stake.

"You okay?" Jim said.

"Yeah," Paul said, "but I have somebody I'd like to bring with me."

"The more the merrier."

"Can you meet me back here in twenty-four hours? Same time, same place?"

Jim smiled. "I can do that."

"Promise?"

"Cross my heart," Jim said. He reached out and lightly squeezed Paul's arm. "I got a feeling that you're a friend."

"More than you know," Paul said, putting his hand over Jim's for a moment.

Back inside the restaurant, Paul looked at the menu, then slipped it between the sugar dispenser and the napkin holder to his left. Mary came to the table, her expression wary but friendly. "Well, did he know anything about the notebook?" she asked.

Paul blinked. He'd almost forgotten. "In a manner of speaking, yes," he said, "but it's a long story."

"Paul, it was in *my* apartment. Don't you think you should tell me, no matter how long a story it is?"

Paul smiled. "Absolutely. What are you doing after work?"

She gave him a look that he took as cautious curiosity.

Paul quickly added, "I was just thinking it might be nice to discuss it over dinner. Some place other than here."

She smiled, a warm smile that reached across her entire face. "You getting food for me? That would be a change." She reached behind her neck, found her ponytail, pulled it over her shoulder and smoothed the hair. "I was just gonna walk home and feed my cat." She reached over and touched Paul's arm, then quickly pulled back her hand. "If I don't do that first, he'll begin to shred the furniture."

His heart was racing. "Would you like some company?"

"Hey, it's almost forty blocks. I wouldn't ask anybody to walk that far."

Paul felt his heart sink as he realized he'd lurched into an attempt to explain it without thinking it through first. Maybe he'd even ruined his chance to build a relationship with Mary. He searched for the right words to give her a sense of what had happened without putting her off altogether. How could he explain it all without sounding like a madman? There had to be a way; the best would probably be the truth, starting at the beginning . . .

"Unless, of course," Mary added, her eyes sparkling now, "they had something really interesting to tell me . . ."

# Acknowledgments

My first thanks is to my Creator, who gave me life, and my parents who brought me into this world and raised me. And without my wife, Louise, and my brothers, and my children, I doubt I'd be alive today; I love and thank you all.

For this book, particular acknowledgement is held in my heart for the late Og Mandino, who developed the art form of revealing enormous spiritual truths in a novella. Og, wherever you are, I hope that with this offering you'll smile and feel that I have honored and continued your tradition.

History is clear that in a first-century sect of Judaism there was a vast schism between the men and women who had lived and walked with Jesus (Peter, John, Salome, Mary, and the other disciples, referred to by Biblical scholars as "the Jerusalem Church") and the

followers of Paul, who had not met Jesus prior to the crucifixion. Paul's followers won the battle, and later joined
with the Roman Empire and became what is now the
Roman Catholic Church; but Peter and his group went
to great pains to protect the Jerusalem Church's perspective, history, and the original sayings of Jesus. I
owe a great debt to the many people over the last five
decades who have labored so hard to make available,
in English language, the Gospel of Thomas and other
early Jerusalem Church writings discovered at Nag
Hamadi, and to those from the Jerusalem Church of
ancient times who wrote and copied and protected
from the conquering Romans so much of that wisdom
and knowledge.

As we know from history, in the third and fourth century most of the original Disciple's Jerusalem Church
followers were tracked down by the newly-formed
"Pauline" Roman Catholic Church, which by then was
a state religion. Many from the Jerusalem Church were
imprisoned or murdered, but a few were able to hide
some of the sayings of Jesus, which they had so carefully transcribed for twenty generations, and through
the work of Biblical scholars these are now again available as the Gospel of Thomas. What a gift!

Most of the sayings of Joshua in this book are direct
quotes from the Gospels of Thomas, Matthew, or Mark,
the presumed oldest books of the early Christian era

and heavily influence by the Jerusalem Church of Jesus' original followers.

All of the words spoken by the woman named Wisdom are from the books of Job, Proverbs, Ecclesiastes, and Song of Solomon of the Tenach, also known as the Old Testament. They are among the few places in the Bible where divinity speaks in a feminine voice.

I am grateful to those who have shared this wisdom with me over the years, particularly Hillel Zeitlin, Hal Cohen, and Gottfried Müller. My interpretations and representations of these teachings, however, are entirely my own, for better or worse.

This book originated from a suggestion Neale Donald Walsch shared with me one afternoon in February 1999. He encouraged me to write the book and the next day my wife, Louise, and I brainstormed the outline. Neale and his wife, Nancy Walsch, offered brilliant editorial suggestions to the early drafts: they're two of the finest editors I've ever worked with. Without Neale, Nancy, and Louise this book wouldn't exist, and I am deeply grateful to them all for helping bring it from the realm of idea to the realm of the printed page. Bob Friedman of Hampton Roads also deserves many, many thanks for his role in producing this book.

Scott Berg, Anne Roberts, Julie Castiglia, Tim King, Kerith Hartmann, Jean Houston, Jerry Schneiderman, Rob Kall, Tammy Nye, Hal Cohen, Jill Gatsby, and

Gwynne Fisher read early drafts and provided significant encouragement.

Margaret Morton, although we have never met, inspired me by writing and photographing her brilliant book *The Tunnel* (Yale University Press) about the people who lived under the streets of Manhattan until the Giuliani administration stepped up its war on the homeless. Robert Funk, who wrote *Honest To Jesus* and other works, enlightened me considerably through his research and literary works, as did Elaine Pagels through her writings and her speech at Trinity College here in Vermont. I learned much from the truly incredible book *Jesus Untouched by the Church* by Hugh McGregor Ross (published by William Sessions in York, England). I recommend their books to you.

Jerry Schneiderman has been my guide to and through the oddest nooks and crannies of Manhattan for the more than two decades that he's been my best friend.

And many, many thanks to Stephen Corrick, Bill Gladstone, Julie Castiglia, Michael Kurland, and Jerry Gross for their helping me to write and bring to the marketplace the sounds, sights, feelings, and knowings that live in my mind, heart, and soul.

# Hampton Roads Publishing Company

*. . . for the evolving human spirit*

Hampton Roads Publishing Company
publishes books on a variety of subjects including
metaphysics, health, complementary medicine,
visionary fiction, and other related topics.

For a copy of our latest catalog,
call toll-free, 800-766-8009,
or send your name and address to:

Hampton Roads Publishing Company, Inc.
1125 Stoney Ridge Road
Charlottesville, VA 22902
e-mail: hrpc@hrpub.com
www.hrpub.com